I0741097

The Goddess of Pigland

By Mario Zecca

1st Full Edition
The Goddess of Pigland, Volume 1, consisting of the first three chapters, was published in Kindle format in 2008 and removed 2012 for rewriting into its current and complete form.

Rave Reviews for
The Goddess of Pigland

"Surpasses Tolkien's Lord of the Rings in imagination, scope and execution."

The author would love to get a rave review like the one above in the

New York Times

"An instant classic of literature and the greatest fantasy novel ever written, bar none!"

An imaginary friend of the author's who has promised to read the book and then buy a huge ad in

Publishers Weekly.

"Reminded me of Terry Pratchett's "Disc World" novels, only funny"

A guy that once read an article in the

Herald Tribune

"Robin Hood of Locksley, King Arthur of the Round Table and Conan of Cimmeria are now joined by Forenk of Pigland as icons of literary legend and immortality!"

I thought I'd save some future reviewer a few moments of thinking up a quote to go into a prestigous publication like the

Harvard Book Journal

"The runaway BESTSELLER everyone is raving about!"

I may start a self-promoting publication called

The Fantastic Fiction Book Review.

Preface

I began writing The Goddess of Pigland in 1999 and here I am designing the layout of the book and adding a preface 15 years later. I wish to thank Zo Harcourt, my virtual and possibly imaginary friend and editor for her indulgent support through the last third of those 15 years in the book's making.

Although I find my vital connection to the universe in the self expression of many forms of art, it was in my imagination and fiction that I first found solace, shelter and salvation, however temporary, from the slings and arrows of outrageous fortune that we call life.

The natural world around us and certinly history contain marvels and tales far stranger then any invention, but not so much for a thirteen year old with too little guidance, even though there was plenty of real danger on the streets of the Bronx where I grew up.

Time after time, I was rescued from drudgery, alienation and often my own ignorance by a venture into the fictional, mystical and escapist worlds of fantastic adventure, fantasy, horror and science fiction in comic, movie or book form.

The point is I was inspired by many writers and it is my aspiration that I might do the same for some lonely lost someone out there who might need their own Pigland.

eMZee 2014

Preface

[illegible]

A Warning to Readers

Humans are divided by the boundless desires of the super rich and powerful seeking to strip mankind of every vestige of dignity and even the illusion of freedom by grinding them into ignorant, starving and diseased opponents combating each other over delusional religious myths and preposterous claims of the ownership of nature herself. Electronic media mogul hirelings in the pay of the draconic fascist overlord illuminati force cliched pablum rife with unconscious hypnotic instructions into our neural networks in the guise of "entertainment" and "news."

The youth of the world, robbed of any shred of creativity and free thought, are indoctrinated into robotic drones in the army of corporate mind slaves. The one time bastions of original thinking that were at one time art, literature and science are shorn of innovation and replaced by the entropic restraints of unfettered censorship by the reactionary war mongers who rule this planet.

So what can be done to combat the runaway disaster of decline that promises a dystopian future making Orwell's vision of an individuality crushing totalitarian state in his novel, 1984, seem like Disneyland?

The text of The Goddess of Pigland contains encoded subliminal messages that will undo the Machiavellian mesmerism wrought by the puppet scientists operating the hypnotic induction satellite apparatus for the Earth's super rich dictator overlords. The cryptic autosuggestion contained in the pages of The Goddess of Pigland frees the mind of the brain washing propaganda inculcated and conditioned into our thought processes. The Goddess of Pigland undoes the constraints of the imagination allowing individual originality and initiative. The Goddess of Pigland contains arcane script, that when read aloud, negates the ensorcelling harm wrought by the inhuman minions of those who shall not be named.

The Goddess of Pigland may cause headaches, drowsiness or constipation. Do not read if you or a loved one have recently had a heart condition or other serious medical conditions. Ask your doctor or a certified practitioner of astrology if The Goddess of Pigland is safe for you.

Illustrations and Glossary

Page [illegible]
Page [illegible]
Page [illegible]
[illegible]
[illegible]
[illegible]
[illegible]
Page [illegible] Soul, New [illegible]
Page [illegible] Learning to the Quiet Mind
Page 73 Black Earth Singer – Salting song for [illegible]
Page 79 [illegible] Down [illegible]
Page 93 The Terrible Queen
Page 113 The Squirrel Sword
Page 137 Demon Altar
Page 149 The Cage – form of the [illegible]
Page 155 [illegible] Here [illegible]
Page [illegible] and The P[illegible]
Page [illegible] of the [illegible]
[illegible]
[illegible] The Glossary [illegible]

1 A Birth in Pig Whistle

It was an ordinary mid-afternoon in the grimy and foul smelling village of Pig Whistle. The rare visitor, overcome by the brutal assault upon his sense of smell, took little notice of the sounds swirling around the filthy hovels and pigsties scattered here and there in no particular order.

Today, however, an irritating shrill came from one of the farm homes, and that nerve-wracking muscle-clenching newborn-baby scream distinguished itself by bringing the familiar pig oinks, farmer complaints and pig-milkmaid murmurs to a halt. Grimacing faces turned their attention to the hut of Mojka, the village's unofficial fortuneteller and crazy person.

In that particularly muddied hut, the official village astrologer, Floob, conferred with Mojka to determine if the infant's birth was auspicious on some way.

Mojka, the mother of the child, insisted that her child was of the divine persuasion, as most mothers are wont to presume. She sat up in bed, cradling her newborn son, still covered in mucilaginous afterbirth. The child cooed strangely. The elderly wise man, Floob, consulted the tools of his trade, a pig's skull painted with red and black designs signifying various arcane powers, stones with crude runes carved into them and a stick of charcoal with which he marked a pigskin with odd symbols.

Floob rubbed his good eye and then traced motions in the air before him. He spent a moment observing the space in front of him as if he could read what his hand had just traced there. He blew his nose loudly in the general direction of his long-sleeved robe and said, "My dear Mojka, I have studied the stars and the three visible moons this week, I have watched the sun and clouds in their paths, the flight of fowl, consulted with the spirit world and in silent prayers asked the Pig Goddess Thegotta for a sign. But I have received no omen, heard no mystical voice nor received a portent signifying a momentous event."

He paused un-meaningfully and then said, "To all outward appearances this is a normal birth, ahem, even average, if I may say so. Now, if the boy were to be born four nights hence, that would signify something…"

"HE IS SPECIAL!" Mojka said.

Cut off sharply, Floob was startled into silence.

"Believe me, I know," Mojka continued, wiping a fleck of Floob's snot from the baby's forehead and onto the bedclothes. She looked up at the soothsayer, her eyes almost wild and said, "Was he not born at around noon, on this tenth day of the first month in the Year of the Pig?"

"Yes, that is right, and the significance of that being?" Floob asked.

Mojka's husband Kormed interrupted them from the other side of the bed where he stood gazing at the child and announced, "He is not half bad looking either, although I cannot imagine where he got his looks from." Kormed laughed uneasily and joking asked Mojka, "You haven't been round to see Toobang the Tanner have you? I hear he's a real terror with the ladies."

Kormed had been flabbergasted to find himself a father upon returning home from tending the pigs. It had been more years than he could recall since he and Mojka had shared the intimacy necessary for the conception of a child. Mojka and Floob ignored him, but the baby, who had stopped crying, looked at Kormed and commenced sobbing again, wailing with the anguish one would normally associate with a tortured animal.

"Well," Floob the wise man went on as if Kormed had not spoken, "if only we had a clear sign which would reveal the child's fate." As if nature conspired to ignore Floob's request, an ordinary cloud passed before the sun causing the room to grow only a shade darker. A common bird cawed in the distance and the child broke wind that sounded wet. Floob's eyes widened incredulously and he frantically scribbled something on the pigskin. Gathering his instruments of divination, he disappeared through the opening in the wall that served as a door. Mojka and Kormed looked at each other and something that bordered on but did not quite achieve comprehension, flashed between them.

Kormed looked down at the screaming babe and said, "What name will you give the boy?"

"Forenk," cooed Mojka, rocking the child gently in her arms, "His name is Forenk."

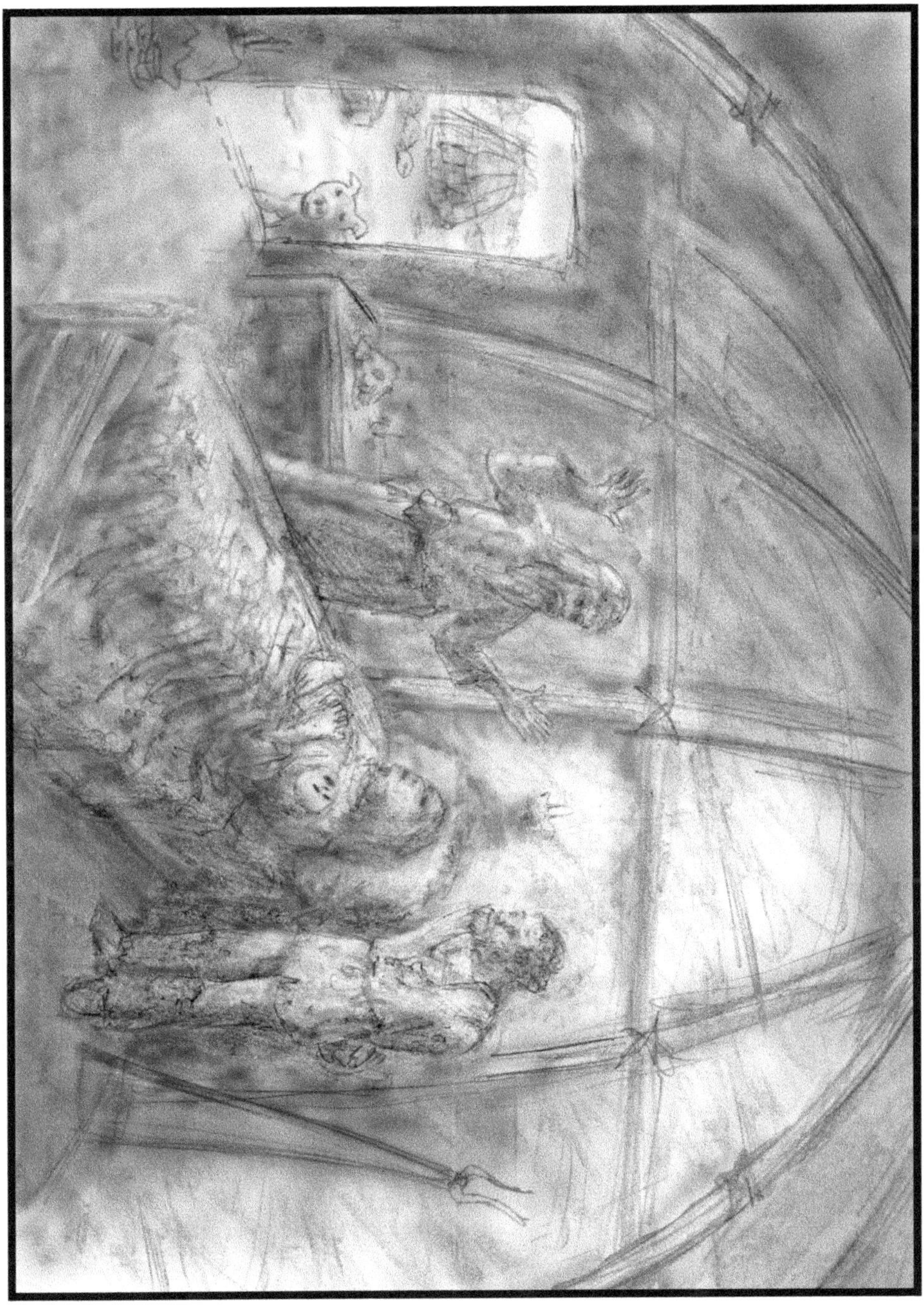

His Name is Forenk

2 The Cursed Son

Time passed and the child grew and started his journey of exploration of the world and everything around him. One thing that grew to be apparently unapparent were his parents. If they were bent over their tedious daily tasks, Forenk was challenged in telling them apart, for they were equally odd in their appearance being squat, ugly and covered from cowlick to fetlock in pig manure. Bathing, frowned upon not only in Pig Whistle but in greater Pigland and the surrounding environs was distrusted and banned as blasphemy.

Forenk's father, Kormed, often joked that some other couple must be Forenk's real parents, for his son was merely plain and dull looking, not vile and malformed like he and his wife, though he did have the family smell. Kormed had entertained the possibility that someone else was responsible for fathering Forenk, but a glance at Mojka usually banished that line of reasoning. Since he had not actually witnessed the birth, he often shared his alternate theories with Forenk.

"Sure enough, Forenk, you re a foundling child, a changeling left by some whimsical god or perhaps a king who will come to claim you after his throne is secure!" Then Kormed would take a good look at Forenk and before turning away add, "Or..., some ordinary folk who did not want the responsibility."

While Kormed's whimsical theories were entertaining, Forenk soon recognized that accidents seemed to occur wherever he went. He was a veritable shuffling disaster, leaving in his wake a path of destruction far beyond the familiar laws of coincidence. It seemed completely improbable, totally impossible for one person to be present at the site of so many mishaps and havoc. Some mysterious force was surely at work.

In the beginning, there were only minor injuries: bumped heads, stubbed toes, twisted ankles and the occasional septic laceration or the odd internally bleeding contusion. But as

Forenk grew into early manhood the property damage, fires and permanently disabling injuries began.

The first serious misadventure involved a stone-laden wagon rolling down a hill and destroying the home of the village chieftain. This accident gave the leading citizen of Pig Whistle, Hetman Walla, a near-fatal head injury and a tendency to whistle through his nose when his mouth was closed. The Hetman also acquired a strange twitch that caused the facial muscles under his right eye to bunch up, exposing his teeth on that side and giving the impression that he was snarling. The villagers found this and his disconcerting habit of staring malignantly without saying a word, disconcerting, although they all agreed the chief had always stared like that.

Wherever Forenk went he caused a continual series of accidents, destroying huts, walls, carts and ladders. Almost everyone in town had spent a day recuperating from some impossibly ill-fortuned feat of clumsiness when Forenk was nearby. His name was used in the context of warning, derision or insult. "Even Forenk could do that without messing it up," or, "You Forenk! Why do you not watch where you re going?"

Forenk had become the butt of jokes, the subject matter of town gossip and was referred to by the title of The Cursed One. Forenk's situation became critically serious when he mistakenly poisoned the town's drinking water, causing more than a few deaths, livestock and domestic pets for the most part. Forenk had been working with the town work crew digging a latrine, commencing at the center of town and diverting the rank muck and offal from the public privy and hazardous waste from Toobang's tannery, to the nearby river. Somehow the crew managed to have the canal empty into the river upstream from the section where the townsfolk collected drinking water. No one bothered to ascertain how the miscalculation had occurred, everyone blamed Forenk, and considering his history, it was understandable.

3 Mojka the Mad

The destruction of tools and belongings was bad enough but the loss of livestock and family pets, not to mention a couple of unfortunate folk, was too much for the citizens of Pig Whistle to bear. With makeshift weapons in their angry hands they stormed up to the sty-yard facing Forenk's hut calling for Forenk's head. The ugly howling was cut short as Mojka appeared in the door hole.

Like her son Forenk, Mojka had a reputation for sheer weirdness. Pigs lifted their heads from rooting for feed and watched Mojka when she passed. She said funny things in conversation with the empty air. Worst of all, while Forenk caused catastrophes, she often predicted them and the townsfolk had learned to obey her warnings to avoid misfortune. Now she warned the people of the village that any harm that came to her son would spell doom for all.

Mojka said, "Take your weapons home, for I am she who is the Mother Incarnate." She studied the dull and grime-covered faces of the townsfolk as their eyes widened or were cast down.

"My son Forenk will deliver this village from an evil fate. If you harm him, the Gods, I among them, will abandon you. Mark me now, in the near future Forenk will leave on a divine quest and return to smite the enemy who would enslave the folk of Pig Whistle. So speaks Mojka, the manifestation of Thegotta, Goddess of Pigs!"

The townsfolk looked around quizzically. Fear mixed with cautious derision in their furtive glances.

Mojka said, "I know to you Forenk may seem a living calamity, one who has caused more carnage than the black pox plague. Think of the misfortunes you have suffered as karma, as payment for the fortune Forenk will bring in the future." Mojka was aware of how easy it was to manipulate the brutishly ignorant peasants of Pig Whistle. A few key phrases spoken with a bit of passion and the mob was diverted from its purpose. She refrained from toying with them and the crowd melted away.

Hiding under the hay-covered board that served as the family bed, cheeks burning with shame, Forenk knew that without his mother's intervention he would not have survived the hour. The townsfolk would have beaten him to death and they had tormented him for as long back as he could remember.

He was sick of being the scapegoat, the butt of endless derision, detestation and violence. Forenk wondered about the preposterous frequency of collisions, spills, smashes, crashes and wrecks and how these incredible accidents seemed to originate from him. He saw himself as kind of a perverse magnet, drawing mishap to himself and pushing happiness away. He thought maybe it would have been better if the mob had killed him.

There was also another matter weighing heavily on Forenk's mind. Although his mother had rescued him from the crazed town folk and he felt a sense of gratitude, she was also a source of embarrassment.

Over the years, she had developed strange habits, regularly making claims of being an immortal, and while most folks feared her, they thought of her as the town loony. Floob the village soothsayer was more business-like and, although also thought of as odd, he was capable of holding a conversation without breaking into near hysterical wailing about being a god. Mojka's lunacy, on the other hand, had granted her a unique standing in the social hierarchy of Pig Whistle.

The uneducated rabble made jokes behind her back but acted warily respectful when her eyes fell on them because they feared her out-of-the-ordinary behavior might be supernaturally inspired. Mojka occasionally made accurate predictions of the future, compelling the dim townsfolk to listen to her screeching inanities carefully.

So from the day Mojka gave the villagers the warning about harming Forenk, they did him no harm physically, avoiding close contact with him. Instead they tormented him anonymously, usually behind his back or from a safe distance.

Several years passed in this fashion, Forenk keeping to himself, and the townsfolk staying clear of him or making jokes of his misfortune when they could do so without being singled out. After a time, when it was realized that their behavior was relatively safe from a distance, the mockery became more brazen and commonplace. And so it went for poor Forenk, the Cursed Son of Mojka the Mad.

4 The Third Eye of Enlightenment

The Grand Pork Festival was the annual carnival and agricultural fair that took place in Pig Whistle. Every village that had a population large enough to make it worthwhile had a similar festival. Without exception, these towns were located along the Sty River which ran the length of greater Pigland. Greater in this sense meant encompassing all of Pigland and not referring to the other definition of great or even good and in fact using the word fair may be pushing it a bit. Perhaps saying throughout all of Pigland would be more precise.

The festival started in Pigmilk, the seaport and largest town in all of Pigland, and then traveled each few days upriver to the next besmirched grouping of pig farms until it came to the last village, Pig Whistle. Pig Whistle was bordered by lands that even pig farmers deemed undesirable.

The people of Pigland found the Grand Pork Festival a refreshing break from their pig farming activities, and, although lacking any vestige of imagination, they found the festival nearly amusing. Often, during the festival, one could see an occasional smile or hear a short laugh, although some of the latter noises might have been grunts or choking sounds.

The point is, the festival was a high point and big deal for the Piglanders and if they looked forward to anything, the festival was the one thing that was generally looked upon as not entirely disagreeable. Piglanders had trouble grasping concepts like goals, hopes and dreams. Their philosophy was a much simpler one, consisting of tending pigs, eating, defecating and sleeping.

~”~

The day before the Festival, just after midday, Forenk was going about his duties shoveling pig manure about with his father. Mojka waddled out of their wattled hut immersed in one of her rapturous episodes, which Forenk noted, she seemed to be experiencing at an alarming frequency. Kormed pretended not to notice and continued to push the swine dung around with his stick.

"Darling son, dearest husband, I have a wondrous announcement to make. The primal gods have granted me a third eye to see into the great beyond of the divine realms. Behold, the magical manifest, a miraculous and wondrous revealing of my godly being!" Mojka said and pointed to her forehead.

"It looks a bit like a wart, mother," said Forenk. Kormed nodded in agreement and said, "Looks exactly like a wart. The one you've always had there." "Well, believe me, it is a third eye! The immortal deities who rule the world do not grant warts to their favorites!" Forenk and Kormed stared in pity. It seemed that every day added a degree of derangement to Mojka's behavior. "With the aid of my third eye, I have pierced the mysteries of the world and essence of existence. I have discovered the Truths of Truths." Mojka breathed in deeply and although exasperated with her families incomprehension, continued, "Open your eyes to the wonders that abound in the seemingly ordinary, smell the air, look at nature's bounty, sing and dance, life is fleeting," she smiled madly while scolding them.

Kormed said, "That is a bit of a challenge, being surrounded by a swine slush and all."

Mojka would hear no rebuke. Fixing Kormed with a frightening glare, she said, "Rise above, soar beyond, ride with the wind, sail the sea, live, laugh and love." She turned to Forenk, smiled broadly and said, "There is a huge world beyond this swine shire, son, and I want you to know of the possibilities that exist. You have a very special destiny, a part to play in the affairs of the land."

Forenk began to shy away at what seemed to him an extreme philosophy but the authority in her voice confused him. There was something in him that wanted to believe it was possible, that there was more to life than a reeking pig farm.

Mojka studied the expression of alarm on his Forenk's face and concluded by saying, in a voice more commanding and much louder than normal, "By the eight teats of Thegotta, you shall be enlightened!"

Mojka voice echoed for a moment and then was followed by a sound rising in the background. It was a sound somewhere between an old man clearing a congested throat and a large mammal ridding itself of intestinal gas. Forenk and Kormed's eyes widened as the swine in their pig pen and every other pig in the village of Pig Whistle snorted in unison.

Mojka Reveals Her Third Eye

5 Carnival Jeers and Forecast Fears

The next day the townsfolk were in early attendance, entering the fair ground site even as the sun rose in a cloudless sky. This was a large open meadow within eye shot of the pig farms that half surrounded. The field had been cleared of the obvious shrubbery to make way for a few makeshift fences, tents and vendor's booths that were thrown up at the midseason.

Not long after the first attendants strolled in, merchants began to bark and boast of their wares. Soon after children screamed in excitement at the "Ride A Blindfolded Pig" and the "Beat the Village Idiot with a Large Stick" attractions. The smells of freshly baked, fried and grilled pork-based foodstuffs mingled with the more familiar odor of pig. The Grand Pork Festival had commenced.

The village folk who recognized Forenk hooted as he made his appearance, approaching from his home area of the village and striding into the stubble field with the family show pig Harbo in tow. Many of the townsfolk had been waiting for Forenk because he was one of the main draws of all public gatherings in this large farming community.

Forenk and Harbo walked past the crowd gathering around the entrance banner swaying in the breeze. The banner was emblazoned with a poorly painted swine-silhouette. Children, holding pig pennants painted by the same inexpert hands as the entrance banner, peered curiously at Forenk as he passed. Half-hidden behind their guardians, they snickered or threw pebbles, until they were warned serendipitously of the possibilities of being cursed.

"Do you want the foul luck of Forenk? If you touch him, even with a thrown stone, his curse will fall on you," chided one mother to her child.

"Stand back children! It is only safe watching from a distance," warned another mother to her brood.

The throng stepped out of Forenk's way and followed at

a cautious distance, far enough to avoid being casualties, but close enough to witness and enjoy the catastrophe that would inevitably take place.

A limping villager, a victim of an accident caused by absent-mindedly wandering too close to Forenk, hooted, "Look out! It is the Cursed One, the great bearer of calamity! Beware!" With that the hooter fell in with the crowd that followed Forenk to watch today's performance of misfortune.

Someone yelled an encouragement as if wishing a performer well, "Break a leg, Forenk!" The yeller added a sarcastic caveat, "But pray, not mine!" The crowd responded with a mixture of laughter, catcalls and earnest oaths of dismay. Forenk wandered around the fair with the mob in tow and aware that he, not the acrobat, juggler and sword swallower, was the main attraction and entertainment of the fair.

Distracted by the sights, smells and sounds of the festival, the gawking throng, underdeveloped attention spans stretched to the limit, wandered away from Forenk one by one.

Finally alone and free, Forenk wandered over to watch the livestock judges inspecting the pigs for the breeding competition. After what seemed like a very scant discussion, Harbo, Forenk's family pig, won third prize for breeding despite the competition of two other pigs. One of the judges handed Forenk the prize, a piece of gaudily painted string that left an itchy rash on Forenk's hand.

After disposing of the prize string, Forenk, now mostly ignored by the festival crowd except for the occasional watchful eye, wandered through the fair with Harbo. He spent a few coppers tasting the food wares of the foreign vendors who asked him to stand as far away as possible from their food booths. Anyone who lived more than a day's march away and was seen only few times a year at the festival and rare market days was considered a foreigner, but even they knew of Forenk and the bad fortune that accompanied him where ever he went.

Forenk spotted Floob among the festival attraction booths. Floob was second runner-up for town loony after Mojka. Forenk attempted to stroll past the astrologer without

Forenk Enters the Festival Grounds

being noticed. Floob, however, shuffling through a stack of pigskin scrolls at his fortune telling booth, glanced up as Forenk passed.

“Ahh, young Forenk. You have been on my mind,” the ancient wheezed. Forenk, in a hurry to move on, nodded to the old lunatic with impatient respect.

The wizened star reader said, “Exactly twenty years after the day of your birth I took the time to re-study the reports of important oracular activities surrounding your birthday. I discovered I had failed to take into account& let me see, it was a profundity festival on the anniversary of, of, what god was it? Where are my notes?”

Floob rifled through various pig pelts covered in greasy scrawling, spread pell-mell on his booth counter. After a a few moments he gave up and said, “In any event, I changed my initial prognosis and I hereby confirm that your life is indeed an extraordinary one. Unfortunately, not at all in a way that could be interpreted as propitious. I m afraid you have been burdened with some sort of curse.”

“Yes, wise man, that revelation has occurred to me as well,” remarked Forenk stiffly and turned to move on.

“Not so fast,” the wise man said. He fumbled with his rune stones while consulting a pig-hide document covered with esoteric markings that somewhat resembled the heavenly constellations or a pig intestine depending upon which side it was viewed from.

“I do not think I would be mistaken in telling you that my forecast readings indicate that today is a turning point in your life.” Floob pointed to a few black scratches on the pigskin chart and said, “As you can plainly see, here are the signs of the road, the sea, the mage, the pig, the god, the sword and the squirrel. They intermingle here.”

Floob cleared his throat nervously and said, “In my studies of these charts I have determined that the curse upon you is derived from some long past dispute, perhaps an altercation involving an ancestor. I would venture you have inherited a legacy of a loathsome ilk.” A strange smile crossed Floob's features, as if he had enjoyed pronouncing that sentence. He repeated it, "..Inherited a legacy of a loathsome ilk."

Forenk looked for the images the village seer described in the complex crisscross of curvy lines, dots, dashes and squiggles, but to him, the chart looked like a pig intestine.

Floob interrupted Forenk's study of the chart and said, "As you will discover, the cross reference is unclear, but you are the catalyst, I have no doubt." He put a wrinkled finger on a particularly curvy line, then moved it in a zigzag fashion across the pigskin, "Here you go, then here and there and back again and oh my, what on earth can that possibly mean?"

Floob's good eye slowly swept across Forenk and a look of horror spread over his face, something had upset him. He curtly rolled up the swine scroll and gathered his strange accouterments. "Well, I hope I've been of some help to you. Heh, heh, heh. Have to run off now. They'll be needing me in the, er, other areas of the fair."

"Yeah, thanks a lot. That certainly clears up matters for me," Forenk said, not realizing he was being sarcastically clever.

Floob, shaking his head, turned to hurry away. Looking back at Forenk he said, "Mention the news to your mother."

"Sure," said Forenk. But as he watched Floob depart a sinking feeling overcame him. Forenk felt as if fate were soon to intervene. He did not know that after today it would be a long time before he would speak to his mother or see his home again.

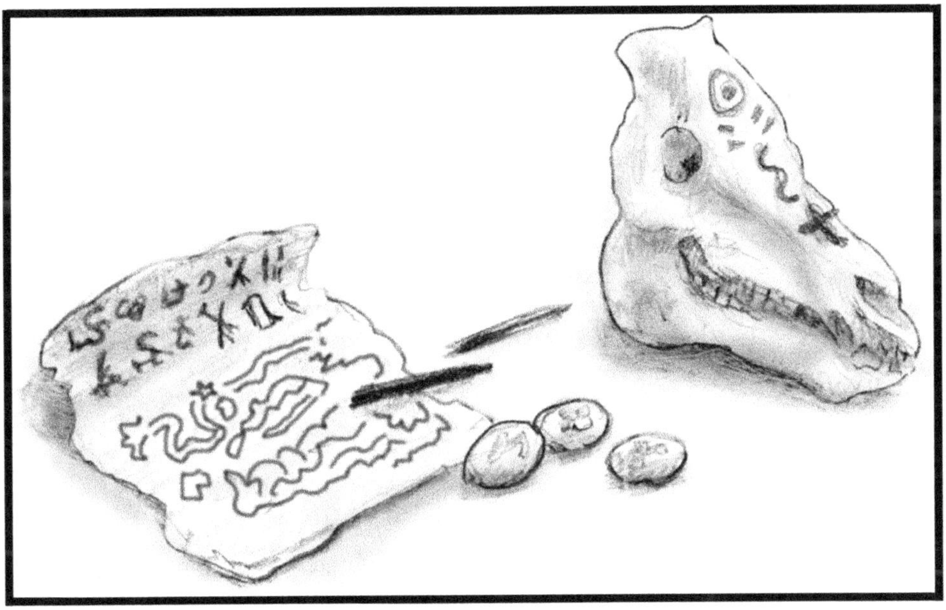

Floob's Tools of Trade

6 Words Before Swine

Of all the festival events, the most popular, and most difficult, was the one-armed pig-in-a-sack race. Participants in the competition climbed into a burlap bag with a full-grown pig and were required to hop across an obstacle-strewn, multi-hurdled course with one hand tied behind their backs.
At last year's event, Forenk managed to come in second, the year before that third.

As Forenk and Harbo walked towards the starting line he considered the progress he had made and felt an unusual sense of confidence. Perhaps he would come in first in the race this year. Maybe that is what Floob was going on about. He recalled that the old astrologer had said, "…inherited a legacy of a loathsome ilk." That did not seem reassuring and Forenk had never placed first in anything except in causing injury and damage. Something would surely go wrong. He or someone near him would have an accident and lose the race. The whole town would despise him and then, after recovering from the shock, ridicule and humiliate him.

Forenk looked back towards the village, wondering if he could sneak home without being noticed. He looked at Harbo, on the other end of the rope tether. The pig looked back. "Mother will never let me rest if I do not take the risk and run the race, especially after yesterday's sermon, right Harbo?"

The pig nodded its head up and down in clear agreement. Forenk leapt back a yard, a freakish flush of fluids flowed as if someone had just changed the rules of reality. Forenk stammered, "Har, her Harbo, do you understand me?" he waited for a reply, but the pig had lost interest and was watching a sow nearby.

Forenk got on his hands and knees, his face just a hair's breath from the swine's snout. "Harbo, can you understand what I say?" He repeat the question, almost yelling until he got the pig's attention. Forenk said, "If you can understand me, nod your head again." Harbo grunted and sniffed at the ground in a very pig-like fashion.

Laughter erupted from behind Forenk. He turned to look over his shoulder to find Hetman Walla, the village leader, and at least eight or nine of Walla's family members, all studying Forenk. Walla's facial muscles twitched under his right eye causing his mouth to open, revealing yellow teeth. Seeing Forenk reminded Walla of the head wound that had almost killed him when he had been struck by a wagon loaded with stone crashing through the wall that had demolished his once sturdy home.

Forenk thought back to that moment and remembered he had in fact been loading the wagon with stone from a rocky hill over looking the Hetman's hut. He had turned, picked up a large stone and when he turned back the wagon was rolling down the hill towards the one stone structure in the village of Pig Whistle.

Then some someone yelled, "It was Forenk, the Cursed One! He was loading the wagon!"

Walla also recalled the incident and he had not been surprised by the cause of the accident. Now, seeing Forenk on his hands and knees talking to a pig, the town chieftain strove for a fitting invective to hurl at the unfortunate village scapegoat. He shook visibly with rage, spittle leaping from his quivering lips, but only a sputtering growl escaped.

The contorted expression on Walla's face and the hostile grimaces on the faces of Walla's family warned Forenk that if there were not scores of people nearby they would murder him on the spot.

Forenk exhaled with relief when the chief's eldest daughter, Floexa, the most attractive female in Pig Whistle, merely ridiculed him. She said, "Forenk Foul Fortune, as if ill luck were not enough, now you talk to pigs, or were you trying to steal a kiss?"

Floexa's jab at Forenk had most of her father's clan tittering in menacing tones. The laughter grew as they all joined in and yet the entire family managed to remain scowling while they laughed.

"No, I, Harbo he talked...," Forenk said. He looked hopefully at Harbo, half expecting the pig to speak in his defense.

A horn blared a few caustic blasts from the far end of the field. It was the signal that announced the one-armed pig-in-a-sack race. Forenk could see his mother and father standing alongside the racecourse with the rest of the villagers.

Hetman Walla snorted haughtily and said to his clan, "Come along now, we have no time for foolishness, nor do I intend to expose my family to the cursed luck of Mr. Foul Fortune here!" With haughty distain Walla's family turned and were gone.

7 The Face of Disgrace

Forenk made his way over to the starting line of the race course. Four other contenders to win the race were arranging themselves and their pigs inside the rough burlap bags normally used for harvest storage. Soon Forenk and Harbo were being assisted inside a burlap bag by a wary attendant who tied Forenk's left arm behind his back.

The bugler blasted the discordant trills that sounded the get-ready. On the second set of blasts, the competitors drew up to the start line. A third squawk and the squad of racers began hopping clumsily across the sloppy sward.

Forenk found himself in third place as the racers came up on the first hurdle, a trough filled with pig manure, a proven incentive for clearing the jump. The two opponents bouncing ahead of Forenk were the same two who had come in first and third in last year's race. A lanky young man of about Forenk's age had the lead and made a perfect leap over the tub of squishy turds. The boy in second place pushed himself too hard and lost his timing. Jumping too soon, he tripped on the lip of the trough and spilled his swine in the shit soup. The lad landed on the other side, dry but disqualified.

Forenk had practiced this jump many times and made it with room to spare. The lanky lad in the lead looked back for a moment, which slowed his gait, and Forenk was by his side. Shoulder-to-shoulder Forenk and the lanky lad hopped, leaping in the same crunch, push up and off, moving fast despite being encumbered by a sack filled with an animal passenger over half their weight.

Mojka and Kormed cheered their son as he inched past the lanky lad and bounded over the second hurdle and suddenly Forenk was in the lead position. The crowd's ecstatic roar of acclamation encouraged his normally timid spirit to a level of optimism he had never experienced. Buoyant energy and clarity of mind flooded Forenk's muscles and mind as the distance

Forenk Takes the Lead

between him and the lanky lad widened.

Forenk thought he felt Harbo, beside him in the burlap bag, kicking off with him when he leapt. Forenk chanced a glance back just in time to see the lanky fellow trip and roll. The last two opponents were so far behind that Forenk could walk the rest of the racecourse and still win.

No time to gloat, Forenk thought to himself. Keeping his pace and closing in on the last hurdle, he could see the finish line tantalizingly close.

Time seemed to slow down as Forenk pushed off for the last hurdle jump. It was almost too easy. But, somehow, Forenk was losing his balance and falling to the side instead of leaping forward. He had started the jump just as he had the others and to him it seemed a perfect example of pig-in-a-sack hurdle hopping. But, there he was, falling down in to the trough, the wooden sides bursting open and Harbo struggling wildly. Forenk was flat on his back, soaked and stinking worse than ever with Harbo sitting squarely on his face, practically suffocating him.

The crowd that had cheered Forenk a moment before fell silent for a very short moment. A few crude jokes and ragged titters broke the spell of quiet and the laughing rose in volume as it spread through the crowd and changed to widespread jeering.

Except for the fact that he could not breath, Forenk wished that Harbo would stay where he was so that he would not have to face the cruel audience in his humiliating state. But Harbo scrambled away revealing a more than normally besmirched Forenk.

A couple of brawny young men from the throng of spectators jogged over to Forenk and pulled him out of the remains of the trough. Forenk was lifted onto the shoulders of the two strapping youths. They proceeded to march him around the fairgrounds. The crowd followed, heckling, scoffing and taunting Forenk with tasteless levity. The coarse and malicious faces of the mob seemed distorted and strange. Their variations of uncouth remarks and lewd accusations seemed endless and between him and the bailey had dwindled.

[illegible] in the bailey [illegible] kicking off with him when he leapt. [illegible] glanced back just in time to see the [illegible] follow him and [illegible]. The last two opponents were still behind that [illegible] could [illegible] with the rest of the [illegible] and [illegible].

[illegible] thought to himself [illegible] his [illegible] and [illegible] could [illegible] the [illegible].

There [illegible] to [illegible] for [illegible]. It was almost too easy. But, somehow, Forant was losing his balance and falling to the side instead [illegible] made him [illegible] the [illegible] was [illegible] to [illegible] the [illegible]

[illegible]

The [illegible] that [illegible] a moment before [illegible] silent for a very short moment. A [illegible] broke the spell [illegible] the laughing [illegible] through [illegible] to [illegible].

[illegible] wished that [illegible] would stay [illegible] so that he would not have to face the [illegible] audience [illegible]. But Harpo scrambled away [illegible] a [illegible] best [illegible] Forant.

A couple of [illegible] young men [illegible] of spectators jogged over [illegible] and pulled him out of the remains of the [illegible] was [illegible] of the two [illegible] they proceeded to [illegible] the [illegible]. The [illegible] followed [illegible] and [illegible] with [illegible] that [illegible] of them [illegible] of [illegible]

Forenk Faces the End

Forenk felt himself being drawn into a nightmare.

The townsfolk's high expectations for entertainment from Forenk had been delivered. He was the village charlatan, mountebank and clown rolled into one pitiful being. It was all in good fun and this time no one had been injured, except for Forenk's pride.

They paraded him around until the mob lost interest and in small groups went off to feed on sausage and bacon fat fritters, gossiping about the events of the morning. Forenk was finally set back on the ground. Only a small boy stood staring at him for a moment longer before wandering off picking at his nose. As soon as Forenk was alone, he turned his back on the festival and ran from the field, tears of shame streaming down his face.

8 Of Bumps and Misses

Forenk trotted down to the river sobbing, the long years of abuse catching up with him. Without looking back, he wandered far from the village on a trail that followed the Sty River to where it narrowed and fell away to a rocky valley the local residents called the Rocky Valley. There the waters almost became rapids and swept away the muck and filth from the hovels and pigsties to somewhere else.

Forenk, feeling chastised and guilty because he could not control his emotions, stumbled along the riverside path on a high upper bank. His head bent in abject hopelessness as he recounted his tribulations. Distracted by his dismal revelations, he did not see the two figures approaching from the opposite direction as he turned at a bend in the trail that ran on a bluff above the river. He collided with one of them and sent her flying over the edge of the bank and into the not quite, but nearly, swiftly moving stream.

Forenk, taken by surprise, stared for the few seconds it took to grasp the situation and then, pointing excitedly, blurted out the obvious, "She fell in the river!"

Forenk's first impulse was to run away, but for some reason, he turned to the companion of the fallen female and time came to a stand still and for the first time that day Forenk realized it was a lovely sunny day. Huge puffy clouds nudged by a cool breeze sailed over the tiny river ravine. Golden rushes and flowering weeds swayed gently in the air.

The world fell silent and his peripheral vision grew misty. Before him stood a young woman whose fantastic and dreamlike beauty far surpassed his understanding. He felt a tingle when her full sensual mouth half smiled and her dark fathomless eyes twinkled. Curling black locks cascaded over her perfectly toned shoulders. She wore tanned animal skin over her creamy flawless skin, The animal skins she wore did not quite hide the incredible curves of her body. The nymph-like creature pointed calmly over the bank to the stream, and said, "She is drowning, get her out of the water."

Forenk Runs into Some New Friends

9 Wet Mounds and Wet Bushes

Forenk sprang into action. Running as fast as he could along the riverbank, he glimpsed golden hair bobbing up and down in the nearly rushing current. The young woman being slowly swept away began to spew water and flail her arms as if she were drowning, but even from the distance, mysteriously, it seemed as though she were laughing.

Practically racing along, he tripped over a tree root and tumbled over the edge of the bank. Even as he hit the water, head first, he recalled that he could not swim and began to scream pathetically. Jolted out of his life-long pattern of passive lethargy, he swung his arms and kicked his feet with ferocious tenacity and, remaining buoyant, he moved in the general direction of the girl who had by this time grabbed hold of an overhanging tree limb and was pulling herself out of the water.

Forenk, expending more energy than it would take to fly, touched the silty bottom of the river, only a few feet deep, and with the girl's help, managed to scramble to the muddy bank of the river. Thrashing about in the rushing water had washed Forenk's garments clean of the more recent fecal coating. Although his clothes were thoroughly embedded with grime the more recent filth had been shaken off by the agitated water he produced while attempting to swim.

Numb comprehension of the folly he had inadvertently committed swept over him. For reasons that escaped Forenk, bathing was a sacrilege in Pig Whistle, a taboo and terrible gainsaying of local custom. If the rumors were correct, his act would bring bad health, ill fortune and an awful hex to the village. Of course he had already brought bad health, ill fortune and an awful hex to the village. He wondered if the town would be doomed by a double whammy of calamity. Some of them certainly deserved it, he thought, but a sudden image of a general uprising of the townsfolk to sacrifice him to the gods came to mind.

Forenk's pessimistic reasoning might have continued if he had not looked up and noticed the dousing in the river had also soaked the young woman of the golden-tresses. Her wet garment clung to her body, revealing her very heavy breasts. She lifted the hem of her flimsy saturated dress to squeeze the water out, exposing a blonde triangle of dripping fur. She giggled when she noticed Forenk's absorption and pulled the drenched dress over her head and tossed it ashore. Smiling knowingly at his entrancement, she advanced to him and pressed her enormous breasts into his chest and pasted her lips passionately on his, then said, "My hero!"

Forenk responded enthusiastically as the lovely angel-nymph fondled and then unbuttoned his codpiece. Together they tore away Forenk's remaining clothes and were naked before they tumbled to the muddy bank, embracing each other fervently.

Suddenly, life seemed unbearably delicious to Forenk. All sense of time and place dissolved in the pleasure of surrender as he explored the unfamiliar crevices and basked in the delightful aromas and tastes. Stars twirled like fireworks behind Forenk's closed eyes and secret voices of the wind hissed endearments and caressed his naked flesh. The muddy bank felt as soft as a bed of clouds and he soared up above the vastness of the universe surrounded by bittersweet flames and peaceful beauty. Slowly he descended from that paradise of bliss and back down to the riverbank. He had had sex before, but never with humans. It was good.

Forenk was slipping into a repose just short of death when he heard a musical voice call, "Hey, are you okay? My goodness that was quite a rescue!" The blonde girl's forgotten companion stood on a hillock overlooking the riverbank. It was obvious she had been watching with approval. She said, "I m coming down to join you." As she climbed down, Forenk studied the dark-haired damsel and decided in a moment of creative exhilaration, possibly brought on by improved fluid circulation, that she could stand a little cleaning up, and surprising himself he said, "If you want to join us, you ll have

Forenk is Introduced to the Outside World

to bathe first."

She stared at him in mock disbelief, laughing as she skipped down the slope of the embankment. Forenk watched with great interest as she stripped out of her leather togs, revealing a most shapely and athletic figure topped by curly raven hair. Naked and jiggling suggestively she flung herself into the water.

With her black hair and creamy skin wet and dripping, she started wading ashore, holding her arms out, offering an embrace to Forenk. He mounted her before she regained the bank. Energetic as a she-panther, she clung to Forenk, spurring him on. In a jumble of kissing and caresses they repeated a cycle of crescendo and climax.

The two comely females surpassed his imagination of what beauty could be. They were the loveliest creatures he had ever seen, especially in comparison with the malformed hags and pimple-covered were-sows that populated Pig Whistle. He thought for a moment of Floexa, the hetman's daughter, and how plain she would appear before these visions of feminine perfection. The village chief's offspring would not be so condescending if she could see him now. He imagined walking back into the village with his present company and the reactions of all those who had ridiculed him.

At some point Forenk could not recall, the golden-haired female joined them and it was almost dark before the wanton three lay exhausted, watching the last glimmer of the sun about to disappear over the tree-lined horizon.

10 Sojourn's Companions

"What are your names?" Forenk asked. The raven-haired beauty smiled in the fading light and answered, "I am Heela and this is Donoxa."

"I do not believe I have ever set eyes on either one of you at the festivals or market days, but surely, it is my good fortune," Forenk almost choked on the words 'good fortune,' but managed to continue, "to meet you both. My name is Forenk."

The two lovelies speaking the words simultaneously, said, "We know who you are. We saw you today, in the one-armed pig-in-a-sack race."

In the dim light remaining, Forenk saw them glance at each other and smile. Their voices melded together as one, they said, "You were winning the race and then you fell!" They laughed daintily in unison.

Forenk was not sure whether to join in the laughter or to cry. The sun was gone now, but no cloud blocked the light of the three visible moons. Their orbs shone down in red, green and white.

In the darkness among the trees, the girl's silhouettes were as indistinguishable as their melodious voices. One of them said, "The pig sat on your face!" and their laughter broke out again, echoing through the shallow ravine, the laugh rose into high-pitched peals of whinnying titters. Forenk failed to detect any hint of kindness in the laughter. He felt a familiar emotional betrayal. Accustomed to malicious humiliation, he stood and begin to dress without saying a word.

Sensing Forenk's dismay Heela and Donoxa sprang up and encircled him in an embrace from both sides. The velvety warmth of their double hug and quadruple breast squeeze relaxed Forenk's stiff indignity and swiftly drove away his resentment. His misapprehensions and the habitual fear of persecution evaporated in the current of their touch.

The two beauties said, "We are sorry for making you feel bad, Forenk, but it was the funniest thing we have seen in ages." They sounded as one mind speaking through two mouths. "Dear boy, you need not worry, we are your friends, we will never harm you and from this day on we will stand by you, we give our word."

Despite being somewhat unnerved by the spooky way their eyes shone in the dark, Forenk found solace in their words, believed them and felt some confidence return. "Who are you?" He said. There was silence for a moment and then, Donoxa, the young woman with the golden locks, answering by herself this time, said, "If I told you we were sent to help you but must keep it a secret, would that satisfy you, for now?" She waited for his reply.

"I suppose," said Forenk doubtfully. It was growing dark but he discovered that he could see in the luminous glow form their eyes.

Heela, the one with the raven mane, spoke, "Will you trust us, Forenk?"

Looking askance at her luminescent eyes, as they strolled back towards the village, Forenk gulped and said, "Yes, although I am uncertain of what, I mean who, you are, and though you will not tell me all there is know, I will trust you, if you say there is reason. Tonight, I felt a great weight of trouble lifted from me. Even if it proves temporary. It was like opening my eyes for the first time." At the reference, he peeked sideways nonchalantly but could not help goggling a bit at their shining eyes, almost lighting the tree-covered path they strolled upon.

"My mother spoke about opening my eyes to the wonders of the world," said Forenk. "I suppose she meant something like tonight."

They passed into a clearing and the moons shone down while a cool breeze swished through the leaves accompanied by the lonely chirping of a single cicada. Soon they had meandered back towards the misshapen and haphazardly constructed collection of mud, wattle and sometimes manure hovels the residents of Pig Whistle called home.

They approached the edge of the village and crossed the now quiet debris- strewn festival field that Forenk had fled from at midday. They saw a group of villagers with torches standing under the festival entrance banner where Forenk had made his entrance that morning. Forenk felt a knot tightening in his stomach but forced the distrust from his mind. While the men there were certainly not a welcoming committee for him, there was no reason to fear harm from them. When he left, the villagers had been in a jovial and festive state. It was Forenk who had left frustrated at losing the race, bitter at being mortified by the persecuting herd and deeply disturbed by his life up to that point. But the day had definitely turned out for the best.

He was coming back with two girls, beautiful as goddesses, at his side and felt a twinge of vanity. He began to think that life held moments of pleasure and fulfillment, that it was not all an endless pig pen filled with odorous tasks, his parents criticism and unending boredom broken only by illness, freak accidents and the homicidal loathing of others. There was joy, freedom and hope, the pursuit of dreams and maybe even a quest for meaning, and most of all, there was love.

As they strode into the light cast by the torches the villagers held, the town folk turned towards the threesome in surprise. Forenk recalled that he was very clean, and had bathed.

"It is the Cursed One, he has returned," said a villager, announcing them. Another stooped and shabby villager said, "He looks very happy." Forenk beamed until the townsman finished his sentence, "with his two demon concubines. They have been gone long enough to imitate the beasts in the devil's own rite!" "Unwed fornication with demons!" a third cried. "Look they are clean! They have bathed," another added. "Kill the blasphemers," yelled one of the men, picking up a rock larger than his fist. Then the villagers charged. As Forenk ran, with the girls not far behind, thrown stones whizzing past them, he thought to himself that the villagers of Pig Whistle were a surly lot, not requiring much provocation to become violent. At least they looked like the villagers of Pig Whistle. It was hard to tell because like everyone Forenk had ever seen up until a few hours ago, they were covered in pig manure and hard to tell apart.

11 Great Discoveries

The incensed pack of town folk gave up the chase after thirty paces, too frightened to pursue Forenk, Heela and Donoxa into the dark of the squirrel-haunted night. The fleeing trio worked their way back to the Sty River in the dark, the girls laughed most of the way. Forenk was mostly confused, wondering if he would ever be able to return home, but so exhausted he collapsed into sleep on a soft sward of grass. He slept soundly in the idyllic surroundings, dreams of frolicking with naked dryads in the forest's dappled beams of day swirled through his mind.

Sunrise the next day found Forenk no more than an eighth of a mile from Pig Whistle. He opened his eyes and for a moment forgot where he was. Looking around he saw that he was still in the woodland, lying on a bed of soft grass and best of all, on either side of him slept an exquisite specimen of maidenhood, starkly naked and almost too gorgeous to be human. As he watched, Donoxa opened her eyes and smiled luxuriously. The morning sunlight animated her tousled golden locks.

She turned to Forenk and said, "Good morning. You look well rested. I slept deeply too, but my goodness, I seem to have worked up an appetite last night, I am very very hungry."

"Me too, very very hungry," said Heela. "Well, we have water nearby, at least."

Heela rose and shook out her curly raven tresses. When she noted Forenk's attention, she bent forward and kissed him on the crown of his head, her large firm breasts pushed into his face. Her hands slipped behind his head as she stood up, her waist now equal to Forenk's head, she pressed on the back of his head pushing Forenk's face into the woolly center below her stomach.

Forenk felt the strength in her hands, but did not resist this agreeable coercion.

"Would you like to go for a swim, Forenk?" Heela asked.

Forenk said, "Mmmurphee freeb.

Heela laughed and relaxed her grip on the back of his head although he had not struggled to get away.

"Wonderful idea," said Forenk.

After a dip in the river, the threesome rolled around in the morning-shaded, grass-padded haven. Afterwards, they collected their clothes and prepared to leave.

"We cannot return to Pig Whistle because we will be maltreated by the mob that pursued us last night. Let us follow the river trail towards the city of Pig Milk." said Forenk. "There we can decide what to do, maybe even leave Pigland. I have heard that you can leave to find fortune and adventure. There boats in Pig Milk that sail upon the sea. I should like to see the ocean. I have been told that you can look out as far as the eye goes and not see land. I think mother would approve."

The girls gasped and together they said, "How courageous! You will leave home without knowing what the future holds? Without knowing where we will go or what we will do?" Their words were recited as precisely as a well-rehearsed choir hymn. They looked at each other, angelic grins playing on vixen features. They answered the question themselves, "Yes."

Forenk was amused by their extraordinary method of speaking, puzzled by the oddness of their speech. Something very mysterious was going on but he suppressed the urge to ask, afraid of the answer he might receive.

After a hurried breakfast of pig trough leftovers stolen from an unsuspecting pig on the outskirts of Pig Whistle, they started down the road towards Pig Milk, the sea and a life of adventure.

The traversing trio trekked for days, tromping the path that ran parallel to the Sty River and alongside the pig farming communities that lined both shores of the river. They passed hamlet after hamlet whose mainstay and economies rested on some or all parts of the pig and the pig related. There were small villages named Bacon, Sausage, Rind, Pig's Feet, Pig

Hide, Pork, Pig Ears, Pig Nose and Pig Butt.

As they passed the tiny village of Pig Butt, Forenk said, "Pig butt is considered a great delicacy among the Piglanders."

"Especially the men folk," said Heela. She and Donoxa chortled at the joke and a minute later Forenk laughed.

12 The Road Less Travestied

They disguised themselves shortly after setting out in the mornings by covering themselves in pig muck so as not to be recognized. The disguise worked, for none paid heed to them in the communities they passed through and they were able to take freely from any unguarded garden, food store or pig troughs along the way.

The pig farming communities they passed resembled Forenk's home so closely he often forgot he had left his own village behind. He caught himself getting ready to make a habitual turn or expecting a taunt from one of the villagers. The uniformity reinforced Forenk's concept of a pig-centric universe.

He observed the abysmal lassitude in the townspeople as they faced the monotonous drudgery of each day.

Forenk felt, correctly, that he was on the outside looking in. He had escaped from the depressing routine the Piglanders lived by, but had given up the security of familiarity to become an outlaw without a home. But yet there he was feeling at home, the paradox actually caused a small pain to run through Forenk's brain.

Most of the days they spent traveling along the river and past the stinky villages of Pigland, Forenk felt free, happy and more alive than he ever had before. At times, he skipped merrily along with the girls or walked holding hands, one on either side of him, as they trod along the trail.

If the days were merry, the nights were delightful. No sooner would the sun disappear than the erstwhile journeyers would seek sanctuary near the river and make a ritual of washing away the foulness of the day and afterwards they would do what came naturally.

Free from the close-minded fanaticism that ignorance inevitably inculcate, Forenk had discovered that people are generally more attractive and better smelling if not covered in animal excreta. He came close to having a revelation on the subject of hygiene, and who knows what lofty notion he may have grasped if he had not been distracted by Donoxa's pendulous breasts as she bent over to wash away the road grime at that moment.

~"~

Pig Whistle was the most isolated and remote village in Pigland. It was the last village in a ragged line of hamlets running parallel to the river stretching westward from Pig Milk, the capitol of Pigland by virtue of it's access to the sea and trade which had swollen its population. It took a week of marching for the three to reach the outskirts of Pig Milk.

The first sight of the town was something of a disappointment, for it seemed to Forenk like a larger, and slightly smellier, version of Forenk's home village. The same squat domiciles lined streets that were a little more crowded than at home. Everywhere he looked, he saw the same pig farmers and pigs covered in gray slime, virtually indistinguishable from one another in appearance and odor.

As they walked deeper into town and towards the sea, the spaces besides homes shrunk until they were walking on a road through a forest of homes. Forenk noticed a couple of residents pulling and pushing a cart. The two men were pig muck free, even though they were grimy, un-bathed and smelled horribly of fish. Forenk sniffed the air with a look of surprise.

"Fishermen," explained Heela. Forenk grimaced as they passed the cartload of drying fish that had been sitting in the sun for hours. "I know the smell. We occasionally have fish in Pig Whistle," he said, faintly defensively, "I just never smelled so much of it in one place." Except for a few unpleasantries Forenk was enjoying his adventure and his elation blossomed when he caught a glimpse of the shimmering sea at the edge of town.

Several long wooden piers jutted from a wooden

boardwalk then spanned a sandy beach and extended far enough into the surf to accommodate sea-going vessels. They could see men busy on the docks and a few ship of various sizes at anchor.

Forenk and the girls stepped off the boardwalk and onto the sand and then marched some distance form the ships to a sea-shell littered section of vacant beach front. Then they stepped into the tide and instinctively washed off their Piglander disguises in the salty water. They stood holding hands and watching the sun dip towards the horizon and illuminate rose-tinged clouds. Ecstatic, feeling the gentle push of the sea wind, smelling and tasting the tang of the ocean, they watched and listened as the swaying waves rippled gleaming and the wheeling sea birds keened.

13 Sea Scum Comes a Calling

Forenk, lost in a blissful revelation, was caught unaware and distracted by the distinctive and familiar sound of pigs being forced to do something they did not want to. The noise came from the wharf, where longshoremen pushed and drove squealing swine from a large warehouse corral, down the length of the pier, up a wide gangplank and into the hold of a merchant ship.

"The single export of Pigland," said Heela, smiling.

"Those men are harsh to those poor beasts," said Donoxa. Forenk watched the sailors and said, "Perhaps a bit more than necessary. Pigs are very smart and can be reasoned with, in most cases."

"The sailors have seen us," said Heela.

The men loading the ship had noticed Forenk and the girls watching from a distance and broke off from their labors. They spoke among themselves and soon what seemed to be the entire crew congregated on the beach below the wharf. Gesturing towards Forenk, Heela and Donoxa, they talked amongst themselves, debating something. Finally, a group of the sailors approached, and when they were close enough, Forenk could see that they eyed the girls lecherously. There were five of them and although no stranger to brutish louts, he could not remember seeing so dangerous looking a gang. Unshaven, unkempt and wearing unkind leering grins, they were armed with knives and clubs worn in their belts and bandoliers.

They halted a few paces in front of the threesome and the tallest of the group, who wore an eye patch and a tattered broadcloth shirt, stepped forward and speaking to Forenk but ogling the girls, said, "Now then, how much for a tumble wif yer girls, lad?"

"Yeah," said another of the sailors, scratching at his privates, "What will it cost to shag these sweeeeet looking strumpets?”

“See here, I will give you ten coppers for a bit of flesh flogging,” said a whiskered grognard who spoke directly to Heela.

“A silver for the one wif the big tits,” said a fourth mariner, motioning to Donoxa.

“You want to give me money to fornicate with the girls?” said Forenk rhetorically.

The sailors all nodded enthusiastically and the one with the eye patch said, “That’s right, me boy, wet fur pie for the whole crew.” He spoke over his shoulder to his fellow crewmen, ”I say, these two are a couple of real sirens, aren’t they just.”

Donoxa and Heela looked blankly at Forenk and each other and said as one, “A silver each, per man, plus expenses!”

The five foul-mouthed sailors managed to round up the rest of the crew in the general uproar that followed. The crewman with the eye patch suggested that Forenk and the girls join him and the rest of the crew of coarse mariners at the local tavern.

14 Black Thumb and the Windy Rokker

The Kissing Fish, the largest of the town's taverns, was within earshot of the pier. An inn for traveling merchants and those who could afford a few coppers, the Kissing Fish boasted a colorful exterior and a unique wooden sign hanging over the front door entrance. On a black and white checkered background, a purplish fish floated, red lips pursed to kiss. The fish's eye seemed to watch an observers no matter where they stood.

As the group of sailors, Forenk, Heela and Donoxa approached the entrance, one of the sailors, a muscular and tattooed brute, pointed to the sign and said, "I'll shortly be doing a little squishy fish kissing myself, then nodded in Heela's general direction. Circling his powerful arms around her, he licked his lips lasciviously with a long leathery tongue and said, "Oh yeah, I am hungry for some bearded clam."

The other seamen coaxed him on raucously. Heela, however, merely reached around and raised one hand to his chin and pushed causing him to bite his tentacle-like tongue. The sailor leapt back a yard, yelping in pain and eyes watery. The other seafarers found Heela's rebuff even more amusing then his advances towards her and, in admiration, they rudely murmured encouragement.

Heela studied the sailor who had made the advance on her and who now stood rubbing his jaw, although it did not relieve the pain of his tongue.

She said, "You romantic devil, you must be the leader of all these brave and handsome men. I can tell by your witty metaphors."

"My mutt? said the sailor.

Heela turned her back on him, opened the door of the tavern and walked in and the rest of them filed in a discreet distance behind her. Forenk, expecting rapine and general carnage to follow the brawny tattooed sailor's mortification, exhaled in relief. Any male territorial instincts that may have been twitching to express themselves during the short brawl had been suppressed by a stronger instinct of self-preservation. Forenk knew he would have acted, at least protested, on behalf of Heela and felt a certain satisfaction in the way she had so nonchalantly dealt with the situation.

He guessed that his brief relationship with his bewitching companions was to change. Taken aback by Heela and Donoxa's willingness to take part in a commerce that was only whispered of back in Pig Whistle, Forenk nonetheless found himself adapting quickly to the whims of mercurial experience.

After a dinner of pig sausage, squash and fish soup, the girls and sailors, two at a time, went upstairs to a rented room the sailors had paid for. Meanwhile, Forenk sat in the crowded main room of the inn collecting silver pieces. He had a small bag full before long and was amazed at the amount, never having seen more than a few coins in one place before. He awkwardly tended the silver while the smelliest member of the crew, who sat opposite him at the table, watched him smiling. Something about that smile made Forenk deeply uncomfortable although he was not sure why. Foaming liquid ran down the mariner's wiry beard as he drank from a heavy flagon.

Evaluating Forenk's naiveté, the stenchey sailor, leaned over and, in a fatherly tone, said, "If you think that's a lot of loot, lad, sail those little fillies up to the City of Degeneracy and you'll meet with real riches."

"The City of Degeneracy? Where is this City of Degeneracy?" said Forenk.

A fellow at a nearby table said, "Which one?"

The tavern folk burst into laughter, the quip being something of an old but reliable joke in the coastal towns.

His table mate, the stinky seafarer, said, "Aye, we'd be sailing for Eysor straightaway, the very city I speak of, and we d be having room for three passengers."

There was a sudden and ominous silence as if someone had spoken a curse of death. Forenk failed to notice this for he was distracted as the stinking smiling sailor stood up and held out his large and gnarly hand for to Forenk to shake as he said, "They call me by the name of Black Thumb." He held up his right thumb in the way of explanation. It looked normal as thumbs go, maybe a little dry and callused, certainly not black. Forenk nodded as if he understood, thinking he would not like to find himself alone with this Black Thumb. Forenk took the sailor's hand and shook it mechanically.

"Glad to meet you, Mister Black Thumb," said Forenk. They were interrupted by the catcalls of a dozen waiting sailors as a member of the crew returned smiling from the pleasures administered upstairs.

Black Thumb turned to the sailor that had just returned from upstairs and said, "You've loaded your pork, Salty, now go and finish loading the ship's. Back to the docks with you and make sure we re all set to sail come morning."

The sailor winked saluted snappily. He said, "Aye, aye, Captain," and practically danced out of the Inn.

Black Thumb turned to Forenk and said, "You just come down to the ship at first light, with the lasses, lad, and I will take you out to see the wonders of the world. I m captain of that ship. The Windy Rokker she be named and I dare say, you have met the crew." At that he burst into a salty raucous heehaw. Holding Forenk's hand in a sweaty grip, he stepped around the table putting his free arm around Forenk's shoulder.

"Bring us a couple of mugs of that slop that passes for swill, man!" Black Thumb yelled to the Innkeeper. Turning back to Forenk, he said, "Yes, me lad, tomorrow with a good wind we sail for Eysor and beyond. Ah, that reminds me of a wee ditty we used to sing, let's see, I think it goes something like this."

Oh, a sailor's life is a very fine life indeed
What with tattered sails, salt water and seaweed
It's true you always have a fishy smell
But better than eternity in hell
Yes, a sailor's life is a very fine life indeed

Oh, a sailor's life is a very fine life indeed
With a weevil biscuit and all the rum you need
Might be riddled with lice and have bloody gums
and my bunk mate riding in the crack of my bum
but a sailor's life is a very fine life indeed

Forenk found himself waking from a mild dream of adventure by the cringe-causing singing of a drunken old sailor singing drunken old sailing songs that rang discordant in his ears. He felt himself sinking into nauseous shock as a new set of incredibly offensive sounds and smells assailed his nostrils.

Black Thumb Sings a Sailor's Song for Forenk

15 Baleful Pail Fulls

Several days later Forenk was recounting the many new discoveries he had made on his first sea voyage. The greatest was his intense revulsion to the swaying movements of the ship caused by the rocking of the sea. The second was that Piglanders were not the only putrescent, socially offensive and deeply ignorant folk in the world, and that by comparison, with certain sailors for instance, were not so bad at all. All this passed through his mind as he leaned over the rail of the ship retching convulsively while below the water splashed and seemed to frolic playfully.

Donoxa and Heela were below deck, on service call for the enjoyment of the crew. This, as it turned out, was an all day and all night job. He had hardly seen them since they set out on the open sea. Why they had accepted the invitation to pleasure a ship full of reeking drunken sailors escaped Forenk. On the other hand, it occurred to him that the girls pleasuring the crew and making them happy was a good thing, for surely their normal disposition leaned towards ill-mannered drunkenness and casual murder.

Then there was Captain Black Thumb and his unpleasant and unwanted advances. For a couple of days, Forenk had been able to avoid the Captain, whose breath had an uncanny resemblance to porcine flatulence. Forenk had the sole privilege of sleeping on the uncovered deck of the ship's bow, apparently because of a shortage of hammocks or space below deck. He did not mind staying as far away from the crew as possible, it was only rational thing to do, after all.

The night before, however, it had started to rain heavily and an icy wind had blown down from the North and blown sharp and cold. Captain Black Thumb had come swaying out of his cabin and offered Forenk a dry spot within. Forenk had given in and allowed the Captain to lead him inside the dark wooden room and remove his wet things so they could dry by the stove. It was soon afterwards that Forenk learned the reason the Captain was called Black Thumb, although thumb was imprecise.

The following morning Forenk had been unable to sit properly but eventually found his sea legs, vomiting only occasionally, when the swells rocked the ship and his stomach at particularly steep angles.

His stomach empty, Forenk was able to overlook a slight dizziness and appreciate the beauty of the day. A hearty breeze blew beneath a clear blue sky, snapping and filling the sails of the Windy Rokker. Stories of adventure, his mother had told him, floated up from the depths of his memory. Forenk recalled the tales of the heroes and their adventures at sea, and now, here he was, adventure bound, on a sailing ship at sea headed to…, who could say? He looked out towards the horizon and inhaled deeply. The call of the sea called.

The ship creaked as she made her way through the waves with flapping sails. Forenk could smell and taste the salty air and feel the ocean spray on his face. He heard the waves slapping the hull and felt the craft riding upon the dark unyielding depths and was suddenly sick again.

Forenk leaned over the gunwale and studied the dark planks of wood curving around the sides of the ship and wondered how the ship builder had managed to find trees in that shape when some movement in the water caught his eye.

As he watched, several of the whitecaps of the undulating waves that broke the surface grew arms and those arms began to wave to him. He turned his full attention to the forms coalescing into a group of women swimming easily on the rolling waves. Their long tresses were the colors of the sea, green and blue, clinging to white skin as translucent as the breakers they rode. They drifted closer and he could see they possessed the voluptuous proportions of goddesses like his new companions, Heela and Donoxa. Transfixed by the supernatural allure of the friendly water ladies, the thought that he might be imagining them teased at the edge of his mind.

An uncanny chill rippled through him when one of the

sea nymphs called to him. She said, "Forenk, father of gods to be!" Her voice tinkled like an echo of a pealing silver bell and he perceived the sound in his mind more than heard it which added to the feeling that he was dreaming while wide-awake.

Leaning over the side of the ship to see more closely he saw one of the unearthly sea urchins lips move and he heard the ethereal voice again. She said, "Forenk, come and make loving play with us."

Another of the sirens said, "Fill us with the divine seed, make us all with godly child."

This time he had the sense of hearing the voice in his groin.

It was obvious that the cosmic hands of fate were at work. He knew Heela and Donoxa were more than ordinary mortals and these briny maidens resembled them. Had not his mother told him repeatedly that he was destined for legendary doings? He himself would be a legend. Forenk, lover of sea nymphs, consort of the gods!

He was startled out of his reverie by a giant wave that washed over the side of the ship, emerging somehow from the gently rocking sea. The resulting splash blinded Forenk for several moments and when he looked again the white ladies of the sea were gone.

Had it been a dream?

Frothy salt water rolled off the deck of the ship and dripped from his sodden head and shoulders. Forenk stared at the shimmering blank foam dejectedly. Perhaps he, Forenk the pig farmer's son, was meant to be merely a spectator of legend, a witness to the great deeds of others. He looked heavenwards for a sign that would support the evidence, making up his mind that if he got a sign, he would accept his fate.

As if in answer, an amazingly huge seabird, passing directly overhead, squawked loudly and Forenk watched hypnotized as the bird dropped what seemed to be a gallon of gull guano, fifty feet, with pinpoint accuracy on his upturned face. The impact knocked him off his feet. As he sat there with greenish-white sticky paste slowly dripping from his head,

Forenk felt the avian mutant had deliberately aimed at him. There was no mistaking it, he had glimpsed destiny's strangely complex pattern. A sign had been given to him and the meaning was clear. His destiny was to be humiliated and misused by the world.

16 Mormoomi of the Sea

As Forenk washed bird shit out of his hair with a bucket of seawater over the gunwale, a movement upon the water caught his eye. A wave cap acted suspiciously and then formed itself into a woman as it drew closer to the vessel. This newly formed creature had sea green skin and curved ram's horns jutting out of jet-black curls that cascaded down to pumpkin-sized breasts. A large fish tail broke the surface behind the strange woman of the sea. Forenk thought she must be a mermaid, something his mother had once told him about. Women that were half fish. Or she could be riding a very large mackerel. He could not tell from where he stood gaping stupidly at her.

"Forenk, hero to be!" said the green-skinned sea lady. Her voice was like an echoe of a silver bells only louder and a little threatening. Her voice caused his crotch to vibrate. She said, "Hail, Forenk, propagator of the Mud God's seed!"

Forenk ignored asking what she meant by that and instead he said, "Excuse me, but did you see some sea nymphs?"

The horned green-skinned sea woman looked displeased at this and said, "The prophecy hinted you were a bit slow. Remove that doltish expression from your visage." She waited until Forenk managed a sheepish grin and said, "Good, that's better!" In a milder tone of voice she said, "Now come to me, hero to be! Bearer of the sacred seed."

"Should I jump in the water?" asked Forenk apprehensively, assuming she spoke to him since no one else was around. It seemed to be getting chilly and she did have green skin and horns and seemed kind of moody.

"Gods, you are a dense one. Yes, jump in the water and come to me!" she said.

So, with hardly more than annoying hesitancy, Forenk obeyed and climbed gingerly over the rail and let himself hang

Forenk Dives into the Sea

by his arms before letting go and diving into the cold water. In that instant Forenk panicked for he suddenly recalled that he could not swim. Down he sank into the murky murkiness and when he could no longer hold his breath, he started to scream as his mouth filled with salty brine.

He was greatly relived to find he somehow breathed and quickly recovering from the horror of drowning, he was startled by a whisper in his ear.

"You will get used to breathing water after a time." He turned to see the green woman sitting atop a huge mackerel. Forenk wondered how he could see so well in what was becoming complete darkness.

"It's my magic, I cast a spell so you can breathe water and see in the sea, as it were." said the green woman of the sea. "Hoo…, who are you?" said Forenk, hypnotized by the sheer queerness of this queenly looking nereid and sinking into deathly shock from experiencing a nearly near-death experience. "How deh…, did you know what I was thinking?"

"I am the Goddess Mormoomi of the Sea, daughter of Simori, she who is called the mother of rivers and Tahleos, the Star God, Father Fate! I have come to you as messenger for Tahleos the Star God! And to collect some of the divine seed." Mormoomi spoke in an eerie cadence that reminded Forenk of his mother. Mormoomi said, "Tahleos sees the paths of lives and has decided to favor one who is smiled upon and guided by the supernatural powers of the immortal shepherds."

"Oh dear, listen to her, goddess of this and god of that," said the mackerel interrupting Mormoomi. "Beware, Frenk or what ever your name is, I was once favored by the... oooohgggg!"

Forenk, mildly delirious, still found it astounding and clearly threatening that Mormoomi's dainty green foot had been able to kick the huge fish out of his vision so easily fast.

"Never mind him," said Mormoomi, suddenly in front of him, her spectacular breasts pressing against his chest. "He is jealous of you and does not appreciate the honor I gave him when I made him my mount." She smiled and Forenk grew intoxicated by her luscious beauty.

"Now, a sensible young man such as yourself would enjoy being a mount for Mormoomi, would you not, my hero?"

The thought somersaulted pleasantly through Forenk's imagination and he felt the heat rising in his body considering the prospect. Additionally, there was a vibration emanating from the zaftig goddess that warned him that his answer should be positive and enthusiastic. He nodded his head up and down, like a child being told he can go out to play if he promises to behave.

"Hahaha, I guessed you might," she said, her thighs wrapping around Forenk's hips. He was startled to find himself naked and obscenely responding to the sensual movements of her body. "Oohhaahhh," Mormoomi sighed and the sound reverberated pleasure sonically.

"Ooohhhh, remind me later, I have to oooohh... to give you aaaaahh.... a prophecy!" she said.

Hours passed and it became darker as they went at it like loved-starved manatees. Without breaking stride, Forenk watched as a quintet of nymphs like the ones from earlier in the day emerged out of the greenish gloom.

"We want the divine seed too!" they said, squealing as one. Mormoomi warned them off, "Wait, little sisters, the Pig Goddess's son is mine for now!"

The nereids waited while Forenk, proudly picturing himself as the future hero of Pigland, finished up with the Sea Goddess.

When Mormoomi decided she had had enough, the nymphs surrounded him and he obsequiously acquiesced to the prurient passions of the seething sirens.

As they love played the dim greenish light around them began to glow lighter. Faintly at first and then growing and glowing in the volume of aqueous landscape. The light expanded, telling of a new day dawning, just as the last nymph, satiated and shaken, fell from Forenk's embrace.

"He is a hero"! said a voice from somewhere nearby, followed by delicate tremulous titters.

“No, a god!” said a voice whose words sounded like those spoken as in a dream.

Then, Mormoomi floated before him, this time bestriding a strange looking beast with a pointy nose and fins. Mormoomi the goddess said, “It is time for you to leave and catch up to your companions, they play a part in your game of barter with fate. It is my part to bestow a prophecy. Remember these words, Forenk!

Look to the goddess of pigs for a sign
Sword of the squirrel bring home to the swine

17 Resume the Doom

With the Mormoomi's lyrical portent still resounding in his mind's ear Forenk found himself on the back of the pointy nosed fish-beast. Forenk held onto its back fin as it sped through the foamy billows, leaping, splashing and churning the waters at breath taking speed. He guessed the marine beast was more than natural when it leapt exceptionally high out of the water, a jump Forenk reckoned completely impossible. He was positive it was not a normal sea beast when it turned slightly in mid-air on the high arc of a ten meter high jump and said, "Hold tight, I m going to speed up a bit. This observation did little to assuage Forenk's fear or quell his high-pitched screaming as they pursued the ship, still many leagues ahead.

"Eeeeooowww!" Forenk screamed, then he added, "Eeeeooowww!" and on they went.

What seemed like hours of frantic wave riding to an extremely damp Forenk had in fact been frantic hours of wave riding. Longing to be discharged from the talking sea animal's back he was mightily relieved to spy the Windy Rokker. They approached the ship and the water dwelling beast wished Forenk well as it discharged him and Foenk scrambled up the side of the ship.

The bright sun shone down from directly overhead as Forenk, knees quaking and holding on to the gunwhal rail to steady himself, worked his way below deck where a double line of sailors led to his two companions hard at work in the bulkhead servicing the crew. Forenk peered over the heaving shoulders and bare buttocks of a pair of mating mateys and said, "You will never guess where I've been."

Heela and Donoxa, hair pasted to face and neck with sweat, each pushed a bucking buccaneer to one side to look up at Forenk together, gasped for air and in one voice said, "Were you gone?"

18 The Pirate's Plight

"But that is all the money we have," said Forenk in protest to Captain Black Thumb. Persistent and irritating seabird keening added to the abrasive hubbub of the practically busy seaport of Eysor. After a sordid journey that seemed a lot longer than three days Forenk and the Captain stood on a pier of the docks in the city of Eysor as the rest of the crew unloaded the relentless squealing hogs. When a few pigs managed to break loose and cause a dock worker to tumble into the water, a wharf official bellowed a warning to the men herding the pigs, he said, "HEY YOU SWABS, KEEP THOSE SWINE IN LINE!"

The Captain looked down at Forenk with a lascivious grin and said, "Now if you'd like to go back on board for a spell, I know a way for you to earn back a bit of your passage money! You ll be needing a little cash until you get the girls started in business now, will you not?" He winked, blew Forenk a kiss and then licked his lips and said. "So, what do yer say lad, aye?" A long string of noisome drool hanging from his unkempt beard accentuated the proposition.

"You can not take our money!" said Donoxa. Black Thumb turned on her with a menacing stance, "And why would that be, my little trollop?"

"We pleasured the crew for days!" The tone of Donoxa's voice verged on anger, We earned it and you would be stealing from us.

"The crew paid you for your whore's work. This loot is what I charge for passage on me ship. But even if I was stealing it from you?" said the captain snidely, "What will you do about it?"

Donoxa answered in a soft voice, she said, "Steps would be taken to see that you met with justice!"

Black Thumb open his eyes wide in mock fear and laughed, "That's fine by me, I could use a little justice. All the same, your passage is the bag of silver and the boy can earn some money back for you, if he pleases." Black Thumb curtsied sarcastically to Donoxa and turned back to Forenk.

Forenk said, "You want me to go back to your cabin with you for money?"

Heela stepped forward, but Donoxa put an arm out to hold her back and whispered to her. Then to Black Thumb, she said, "You have made a grave mistake today and shown yourself to be naught but a pirate. No doubt others have met with similar treatment." She waved a hand and in a low voice incanted an oath of enchantment.

Blue sparkling will o wisps pranced round Donoxa's fingers and then jumped to Black Thumb's beard, which started to smoke suddenly. In a panic, he beat at his chest, trying to extinguish the fire he imagined. Black Thumb yelped, "Witchcraft!" as he stumbled backwards over the edge of the pier splashing upside down into waist deep water, hurting more than his pride. The crew stopped hauling hogs and general laughter broke out among them and the other workers around the pier.

Black Thumb, spluttering, started to order an attack, but was set upon by a pack of jellyfish that seemed to materialize out of nowhere. Donoxa peered down at him as he flip-flopped out of harm's way, quickened in his efforts by poisonous stingers.

"Bad luck for Captain Black Thumb, cursed from this day on, until you make amends!" said Donoxa, pointing at Black Thumb. He cringed in response to her accusation and scuttled under the wharf and towards shore. The comic sight of the sodden Black Thumb hiding from Donoxa had the harbor laborers and sailors in a state of wild amusement, although a few now watched Donoxa with suspicion. In the chaos Donoxa led Heela and Forenk to slip away from the wharves and into the streets of Eysor.

They walked into the shabby center of town amidst ankle-deep sewage. The narrow streets filled with the base sounds and stinking stalls of shouting shoe sellers and poorly postured pimply prostitutes. Innumerable gawking loafers lined the alleys and doorways they passed, gesturing lewdly. Unsightly children, a slave trader would not have kidnapped, grabbed at them begging for coins and mangy dogs, resembling long-legged rats, nipped at their heels.

Heela, on the brink of sounding reproachful, kicked one of the dog rats away and said, "I would have dealt more directly with that Blackheart."

"And had the whole crew down on our heads," said Donoxa..

Posed more as a question than a statement, Forenk said, "The captain took all the silver." Then as more of a statement then a question he said to Donoxa, "You used some kind of magic."

"I'm hungry," said Donoxa.

"Me too!" said Heela.

19 The Sign

The main thoroughfare of the large town, a haphazardly cobbled avenue, started at the wharf and ran through the center of Pig Milk. Side streets twisted off from the central passage harboring various smiths, food sellers, tanners, tailors and even weavers. The residents of this cosmopolitan nexus wore clothing made from vegetable fiber and not animal hide clothing because it carried, along with a residual animal stench, an association with life less civilized.

At the edge of town the avenue became a dirt road that soon disappeared into the unwelcoming wilderness beyond. No gate or walls defended Eysor because, in her much less than illustrious career, the town had never gotten the notice of potential conquerors. In fact, if it were not located in a commercially strategic spot, the townsfolk would have abandoned the site long ago to loaf in the countryside as brigands or traveling slatterns, for which they were uncommonly suited.

About half way from the anchorage to the edge of town the roadway opened into a poorly planned plaza where the administrative and government centers, and we must allow for the most generous definitions of administrative and government centers, were located. The spiritual world was represented in this, the town's center as well. Eysor had the only temple that anyone in Pigland knew of and therefore it was the theological center of the entire world as far as the locals were concerned.

It was this very temple that Forenk, Donoxa and Heela came upon as they entered the semi-circular square. It sat, lounged would be more accurate, on their right as they approached from the harbor and Forenk, who had a propensity to be distracted by shining objects, noticed it first because of a sun beam reflected off a large metal object in the tower.

As they got closer in crossing the market plaza, Forenk stared in amazement at the temple. A two-columned portico

The Facade of the Temple of Thegotta

shaded the inner facade leading to the ornately, if amateurishly, carved inset doors. A set of white almost pale gray stone stairs climbed to the porch of the temple between the two pillars. Perched atop a pedestal, a block of square-dressed stone that divided the stair, was a large woman perfectly still on her hands and knees.

The enormous naked woman had, as Forenk drew closer and observed, multiple mammaries and the head of a pig. The skin of the statue was the same color and texture as stone stair and temple.

Heela said, "That is the biggest statue of Thegotta in the world!"

Donoxa added, "Behold, Forenk, a likeness of the Swine Mother!"

"It's a statue of Thegotta?" Forenk asked, "Does she actually look like that?"

"She can, or she can appear as a woman or a sow!" said Heela.

"It is a statue of Thegotta, the Goddess of Pigs," said a short unpleasant looking fellow with lice visibly hopping all over him pointing to the representation of the supreme supernatural supervisor of Pigland. The fellow's eyes nervously however inspected Donoxa's chest. Speaking now to Donoxa's buxom bosom, he said, "You must be new in town, lass, how much do you charge?"

"Five hundred silvers!" She said.

At that the fellow managed a quick glance up to Donoxa's eyes and said, "What, that is a bit much, is it not? Why I can have almost any two tarts in town for a copper."

"How much do you have?" said Donoxa.

The fellow rifled in his cod piece which doubled as a purse, drew out some coins and said, "Well, let's see, I have seven coppers."

"I will smile at you for seven coppers," said Donoxa, bending over slightly, enticingly increasing his view of her bounty. The little fellows eyes bulged out of his head and he hurriedly forked over his coins. Donoxa smiled broadly and reached out a hand to stroke his face, but seeing particularly huge lice crawling out from under the greasy unkempt hair and on to his greasy unkempt face, she waved and turned away abruptly. She, Heela and Forenk proceeded towards the sacred sanctum of the sow.

As they approached the fane, Forenk could feel the blood in his veins tingle forcing a discomforting self awareness upon him. His head was swimming with images and new thoughts, Was the adventure becoming too much to bear? He thought of the tableau at the pier. Was Donoxa a witch? There was no doubting any longer that remarkable events were afoot. He tried unfruitfully to make sense out of Mormoomi's prophetic poem as he eyed the statue with awe. Thinking to himself that maybe a prayer of reverence, a sacrifice perhaps and the deity would deign to reveal....

"A sign." said Donoxa.

Heela relied, "What does it say?"

"I do not know, I can not read."

"Forenk, can you read this sign?" the girls said together, sounding like a song long practiced.

Their voices reminded Forenk of the way the sea nymphs talk-sang in unison. Mystified, he reverently sidled up to the sign, a small square of whitewashed wood leaning against one of the pillars. Forenk recognized the dark squiggles as writing, but there his knowledge failed him, as it did so frequently, for he could neither read nor write and in fact could only count to twenty with his boots off, and even then not always accurately.

Squatting in front of the sign Forenk waited for a disembodied voice, a thunderclap or something equally indicative of divine doings. Instead, two feet clad in well worn soft leather booties manifested before him. A body in a rough woolen robe was attached to the feet. He noted the tonsured head of a monk before reacting in horror to the face he now looked into.

Below the monk's plain brown eyes jutted a large pink pig's snout.

The Temple Monk

20 The Bell Ringers

Forenk felt the hair on his scalp rise on end and he would have swooned in a waking nightmare had he not spotted two leather strings holding the swine snout to the strange clergyman's face. It was a partial mask that the monks had to wear in deference to the Goddess of Pigland.

"Are you here about the sign?" repeated the monk, his voice behind the mask pronounced the words with a nasal twang.

Forenk said, "Er…, yes, how did you know?" He could not help but wonder how the fake-faced friar could have known about the sign he was on a quest for. The sign mentioned in sea goddess Mormoomi's riddle-like divination. He recited the prophecy to himself.

Look to the goddess of pigs for a sign
Sword of the squirrel bring home to the swine

He had discovered a temple dedicated to the Goddess of Pigland, and here was a sign, both parts of the first line of the augury. Forenk thought it seemed pretty straight forward, even if it was a mystical coincidence beyond his understanding.

The priest wearing the pig nose mask interrupted Forenk's musings. He said, "Follow me then, the Patriarch, the High Priest of Thegotta is holding the auditions in the belfry."

After glancing at the girls, who nodded encouragingly, Forenk followed the priest past a vestibule and into a large chamber with a pillared gallery on either side. Statues in alcoves seemed to eye Forenk ominously as he passed. The besnouted priest walked towards the far end of the chamber with Forenk in tow and staring in wonder at the high ceiling, painted with murals portraying scenes of gods and goddesses dancing, slaying or fornicating with beasts. At the opposite end of the chamber they passed under an arched doorway and up a winding stone staircase. At the top of the stair the priest pushed opened a door and they stepped out into a circular roofed and banistered belfry. A huge polished bell supported by a scaffold hung suspended in the air under the belfry's roof. Three men stood before the bell, one tall and the other two very short.

The three men turned to look at Forenk, while behind him the priest with the pig snout mask, referring to Forenk, said,, "He is here about the sign asking for a new bell ringer." This was directed to his superior, the tallest of the three men, who stood staring sternly at Forenk from deep, dark eyes above a devilishly pointed gray streaked beard. The High Priest wore a black robe adorned with gilt trim and gold fasteners.

The other two men, shabbily attired and dwarfs by comparison with the High Priest were unfortunately cursed in aspect. Both were burdened with huge heads and eyes that protruded like boiled eggs from their remarkably similar and grotesque faces. One of them was drooling.

Forenk thought about saying there had been some mistake, he was looking for a completely different kind of sign, not employment. But then he recalled how impressions could be misleading, he keep running into the oddest situations and they seemed to be leading some where. So instead of asking to be excused, Forenk held back his anxiety and nodded ascent. His stomach roiled and gurgled and although he attempted to hold back the gas that had been building up due to the unfamiliar diet aboard the Windy Rokker by flexing his sphincter muscle, he farted.

The sound of a horn filled with water was followed by a scent of dead things. The group turned away pretending not to notice, the drooling dotard a little slower then the rest. The pig-snout priest slammed the door behind Forenk after snorting in disgust.

The High Priest, glaring wild-eyed at Forenk, continued nonetheless as if nothing had happened. He said, "THIS," and made a sweeping gesture indicating the surrounding temple, "is the sacerdotal fane of the gods." After a meaningful pause he said, "THIS bell," he pointed to the bell, "is the sacred means by which we call worshippers to ritual meeting." After another longer pause and some glowering, he said, "One of you will be in charge of ministering the conventual tintinnabulations!" He pouted waiting for the gravity of the statement to sink in only to be chagrined by the looks of bafflement on Forenk and the trollish twins.

"YOU TWO," said the High Priest, pointing to the outlandishly crowned twosome, "will ring the bell now, by striking it with THIS hammer." He pointed to a black metal hammer resting in a matching cradle on the floor.

The malformed men smiled purposefully at each other, then bent to lift the bell hammer from its cradle sitting before the giant bell. Two sets of gnarly hands reached for the hammer but their heads met first with a sharp cracking sound. They stumbled back from each other and one stumbled into the High Priest. The High Priest pushed the dwarf away and brushed off the dandruff and cooties the contact. His face slowly flushed red. He looked down at the pair of cranially-encumbered midgets and, barely controlling his anger, said, "How will you ring the bell if you cannot manage to lift the hammer?"

The dwarf that had not stumbled into the High Priest said, "Like this!" He turned to the bell, took a few steps back and ran towards it, smashing his face into the metal surface which resulted in a dull clang. He turned, smiling triumphantly and wagging his ears excitedly while his nose bled.

A look of profound sadness swept over the High Priest's visage. He turned to Forenk, and said, "Why do you not give it a try, young fellow."

Forenk lifted the hammer and struck the bell squarely in the center causing a chime to reverberate on the very brink of average.

The High Priest, with no small amount of relief, turned to the dwarfs, managed a faint smile and said. "The rest of you may leave, we have our new bell ringer."

The large-domed dwarfs began to file out in dejection; bent even lower than the cringing posture they had displayed only moments before in their futile optimism of becoming bell ringers. The dwarf with the nose-bleed stopped, turned and stared at Forenk. The dwarf's features congealed into a mask of raw anger and frustration. Without looking at the High Priest, he said," I rang the bell just as well as this jackanapes." His blubbery lips trembled with rage.

Forenk faced him with a bland expression, waiting for the response he was sure would surface eventually from the mystery of his thinking. The cranium-enlarged dwarf took Forenk's lack of wit as a scornful rebuff and infuriated, his virulence quickly transformed into a savage apoplexy.

The dwarf said, "I deserve the job, I was here first!" Slinging spittle from the corners of his mouth, he kicked violently at Forenk who managed to grab his stumpy leg and push the dwarf away, accidentally sending the smallish offender back against the balcony and over the edge. Before anyone could intervene, they heard a short cry cut off by a bone-crunching thud.

All stared for a moment at the balcony as if the dwarf's unsightly head would reappear over the edge. The High Priest rushed to the balustrade and peered below to where the body lay, ten yards below.

A crowd of passersbyers and temple acolytes were already rushing to the scene. One of the acolytes noticed the High Priest above and pointing to the bloody mangled midget, and said, "Who is this, Patriarch?"

The High Priest said, "I do not know, but his face rings a bell!"

Behind the High Priest, the second swollen-topped dwarf waved his ears menacingly and admonished Forenk, he said, "You dirty rat, you killed my brother, I will murder you and I will be the bell ringer for my brother's sake." He backed up a step, lowered his head and charged like a bull. Forenk dodged to one side as the fuming large-skulled juggernaut swept by.

The dwarf's momentum took him to the balcony opposite the one his brother had gone over moments ago. He was moving so fast that the weight of his head, just clearing the top of the railing, carried him over the side. He waved his arms furiously trying to gain a hold but failed, his yelp cut off by the sickening sound of his body smashing into the ground.

The High Priest, looking at Forenk with an open-eyed caution, walked tentatively over to the other side of the balcony and looked down to the unpleasant scene below. A voice from below asked, “Who is this man, Patriarch?”

The High Priest responded solemnly, he said, “He’s a dead ringer for his brother!”

21 In Winkle Bush a Flowering

The following morning found the intrepid threesome unexpectedly on the road of adventure once more. The High Priest of the Temple of Thegotta had, after much commotion, explained to the authorities the circumstances leading to the deaths of the two dwarfs. The double murder charges, brought against Forenk by a mob of indolent loiterers with too much time on their hands, were reduced to manslaughter and to his great relief Forenk was merely banished from the city of Eysor, never to return, and not, as was the custom for serious offenses, flayed alive and dismembered.

So Forenk and his companions set out under circumstances that left him a little jaded and weary of the odd peccadilloes that life kept presenting them.

They ambled their way northward, destination unknown. To their west lay the Nose River running south from the Eye Sea. A squat forest of undergrowth, covered by dark overgrowth, protruded awkwardly from the bank of the river. To the East, a scrubby plain, an unsightly vista pockmarked and desolate except for an occasional pock or rabid rabbit, stretched unconvincingly to the sea. They marched all day in silence and made a campfire not far from the road that evening.

After eating barley cakes and pork meat that they had purchased with their last few coins, they wrapped themselves up in their blankets as best they could against the cold night air and slept. Forenk, still shaken from the many extraordinary events that transpired lately, had trouble falling asleep. When he did drift off, he slept fitfully and woke yelping from a nightmare where a naked man with a huge pig's head chased him with a reversed pitchfork that grew out of his loins.

The next day seemed cheerier although Forenk stumbled along almost dozing off as they started north under a bright sun. So it went for several uneventful days passed in lackadaisical traveling, gathering wild fruit and nuts and camping under the stars at night. Life settled down into a pleasant routine as they trod along the path.

On the forth day after leaving Pig Milk, the river veered to the West and an ever-widening forest spread between it and the road they were on. They were all in good spirits and a few hours into the march Donoxa and Heela began humming. Their humming shaped itself into a melody. The melody expanded, and as it did, words were added and those words evolved into lyrical poetry. They sang together, word for word, a mournful lay of days of yore, their voices reminiscent of something familiar to Forenk, yet strange.

From a puffy cloud overhead a ray of golden light descended in slow motion and alighted on the radiant faces of Donoxa and Heela. Raised aloft to the heavens, the iridescent light wove a magical pattern about their graceful features although neither seemed to notice. Their skin shone sparkling in the rays of the bright sun as they continued the strange tune in a lilting chime, angelic and sublime.

They through dark foreboding woods
spied huntsmen come a riding
The lovers touched by pangs of dread
in winkle bush a flowering

Colored whorls like ribbons made of sparkling light rippled around Donoxa and Heela as they continued to sing.

Our fate is sealed, my new found love
without a wish for chiding
I think it is our end to come
in winkle bush a flowering

Forenk, walking alongside the singing girls, was only slightly unnerved by the uncanny spectacle being played out before him. His mother had instilled in him an attitude of acceptance and even a sort of meek optimism towards the bizarre and unnatural. He chose to interpret the heavenly radiance that surrounded his companions as a message from the gods that perhaps the fortunes the tragic trio had endured would reverse somehow.

Forenk watched in amazement as winkle bushes began to flower on either side of the trail they walked. He wondered if the song might be a spell song being cast by Donoxa. Too anxious to merely observe, Forenk said, "That is a strange song you sing. It is difficult to understand."

The girls stopped singing at once, mock annoyance showing in their twined expression. "Do you not like the tune?" they said as one. "Why tis a lovely song, pray, what song is it?" said Forenk.

Donoxa alone said, "Why, Forenk, surely you heard the title in the chorus as we sang, Its called 'In Winkle Bush a Flowering.' It is an old lay that tells the tale of a great beast goddess and her meeting and love for a hero of the first clan of mortal men. The song describes how, despite the wishes of the men who hunted them down and slew them, they became the first man and beast to mate, though certainly not the last, as any lad of Pigland knows."

Donoxa and Heela both tittered at the joke. Forenk blushed deeply.

Heela said, "It brings the luck of the Goddess and good fortune unless interrupted."

A bead of perspiration slowly rolled down Forenk's forehead, realizing he had just interrupted the song. "Unless interrupted?" Forenk croaked.

"Yes," said Donoxa, "unless interrupted."

22 The Squirrel Sword

A cloud overhead suddenly blocked the sun. An owl hooted ominously, a cat screeched and there was a violent thunderclap. The three of them had little time to react to the sound of approaching riders when to their left the shrubbery rattled and shook violently and a horde of dark horrible shapes burst out of the woods.

Donoxa's cry of alarm was cut off by Heela's command of caution and Heela's command of caution was cut off in turn by Forenk's pitiful and unmanly scream.

A gaggle of vermin-infested ruffians mounted on horrific creatures charged at them with fiery fetlocks fretting fiercely. The riders brandished almost dangerous-looking sticks and the one who rode foremost among the mildly hellish horde held an ineptly woven shield that looked like it might protect him from a miss-directed weapon blow or a light drizzle of rain.

Heela examined the whooping and hollering intruders carefully as they reined in their grotesque beasts and circled her and the others. She quickly surmised that the malodorous rascals were not mounted on animals at all. Instead, they wore costumes made of woven branches, reeking untanned hides and rotting vegetation sloppily arranged to give the impression of mounts from some eldritch nightmare.

The raiders dismounted, or rather stepped out of the warhorse part of their get-ups, that actually resembled cows more than horses, and stood facing the three wayfarers.

"Nice horses," said Heela, politely disguising but not completely hiding the sarcasm in her voice.

The bandits seemed at a loss as to what action they should take. One of them coughed with what sounded like a serious head cold. The smelliest of the group, the owner of the shield, revived from the reverie he had lapsed into, barked out of a face wreathed in rank and greasy locks.

He said, "I am Dikked, son of Fukked, and this," then

pointing his thumb at the bandit on his left who wore a huge bone stuck in his hair, "is my brother Shidded."

He paused for a moment to collect his thoughts and fuzzy ideas began to resolve themselves but stopped just short of the mark. Constructing sentences with more than three words seemed to be too much of a chore for him, so he stopped trying.

Finally, Dikked said, "And him," jabbing his thumb at the third ruffian who seemed embarrassed at having attention drawn to himself. The group all waited for Dikked to continue, but he was distracted by something in his nose. After a short interval, he said, "We are sentries of this wood."

"Yeah!" said the other two, grumbling their agreement.

Dikked eyed the ambushees suspiciously, his eyes stopping to rest on Donoxa's breasts. He said, "You are our prisoners!"

"You are taking my breasts prisoner?" said Donoxa.

"What about mine?" said Heela, "are they free to go?"

"I have no breasts to speak of, only nipples," said Forenk.

Shidded, the one with the hair bone, which now swayed menacingly in the nest of his dung pomaded hair, stepped forward and addressing Donoxa's breasts, said, "WE HATE PIGLANDERS!"

Her breasts remained silent.

Heela took up the debate by pointing out that she and Donoxa were not Piglanders and that technically Forenk was a former Piglander, banished for the impiety of bathing. She quickly added that it had been by accident after noting the expressions of shock and revulsion in the bandits response to the word bathing.

Shidded turned to his brother Dikked and said, "So, they are not enemies?"

Dikked's beady eyes looked askance frantically trying to conceal his confusion. Heela decided on a more direct form of debate and grabbing Shidded's stick and pulling it out of his hand before he could respond, banged it on his ugly head, sending his hair bone flying and him dodging back towards his ersatz mount. The band of bowlegged badmashes dashed around madly dodging Heela's painfully accurate swinging stick strikes.

Suddenly, out from the same mass of mossy matted mangrove that the mountebanks had made their dramatic entrance from, stepped a tall figure dressed in a strange looking robe. He held his arms aloft, his right hand held a long and inexpertly carved staff topped with a squirrel tail. His bearing and manner was that of an official of ceremony or person of importance, but it could have been self importance for his clothing and general appearance brought to mind someone who might have sleep in a trees for a few months at a time without bothering to wash.

The tall robed stranger bellowed to Dikked and his brothers, saying, "Stop! Halt, desist, cease, quit and proceed no further, for these pilgrims are sacrosanct and must be spared any harassment!"

Startled by the graybeard's intervention, Heela terminated her pummeling punishment of the chastised charlatans and they scattered towards their cow-mount costumes, only stopping long enough to rummage through their saddle bags, have a short meal and then with much adieu, they rode off and were gone.

"They tried to imprison my breasts," Donoxa said to the newly arrived stranger. The shrouded figure stared incredulously at her, his face reddened as an impure thought blemished his otherwise acetic meditations. "Hrumf!" said the sandaled stranger, "I suppose you are here for the Squirrel Sword?"

23 The Druid of the Sacred Grove

Forenk's mind often spun a bewildering web of myriad musings, but this time there was no confusion. The untidily druid, who now led them into the forest through a hidden trail in the general direction of the river, had clearly asked them if they sought the Squirrel Sword. Mormoomi's prophetic poetry had made it clear that the Squirrel Sword is what they sought. Forenk felt that fate was changing the rules of his adventure every new day.

"What is your name, old man, and where do you lead us?" said Heela.

"Men call me Gerojef, and I am taking you to…" said the druid. "What do women call you?" said Donoxa. interrupting him.

Gerojef the Druid turned to scowl back impatiently at Donoxa without slowing his gait. He said, "THEY call me Gerojef as well."

"It is the same name," Forenk said, and laughed. No one else did.

Gerojef turned to Forenk and said, "Of course it is the same name. It is only a manner of speaking to say, men call me so and so."

Heela said, "Donoxa's question is valid, why say 'men call you so and so,' why not say, 'folk call me so and so,' or 'men and women call me so and so,' or even 'women and men call me so and so!'"

"VERY WELL then, FOLK call me Gerojef!" said the druid clearly annoyed. He turned and continued through the leafy shadows, pushing aside sapling limb and variegated vine.

"So where are we going?" asked Heela.

Just then they broke into a clearing where several loafing oafs in motley dress played at whittle sticks, or, with a marked lack of skill, wove together twigs and strips of leather the ersatz cow mounts, like the ones Dikked and his brothers had been ‘riding.’ Apart from that peculiar and perchance pointless craft, absolutely nothing in the encampment possessed the minutest element of interest.

Along with an unusual amount of filth and muck, there stood a cooking fire and a few lop-sided hide huts. The camp settled into silence as those not sleeping, which counted just above half, turned their attention to the strangers. One of the napping men broke wind. Even in this unimaginative setting, Heela’s curiosity could not be repressed and she questioned Gerojef further.

“Kindly inform us of the purpose of the cows these women are attempting to build,” she said.

Gerojef said, “Men, they are all men, and they are crafting HORSES, war horses to be exact, not COWS! Do you see any horns? They are symbolic, in veneration of the ancient knights of the wood, in homage to our hoofed brothers.” Gerojef struggled to maintain a complacent and wise demeanor.

“Definitely look like cows,” Heela said, somewhat less than constructively.

Gerojef, ignoring Heela’s remark, signaled them to follow and crossed the clearing into a recess that led to a tended grove.

Heela said, “How did you know we came for the Squirrel Sword? Why are you helping us?”

“Word came that we were to expect travelers on a quest and we are under oath to aid you,” said Gerojef.

“Who is we?” said Heela.

“I am the Druid of the Sacred Grove, and we,” said Gerojef as he motioned back to the others in the camp, “are the guardians of the grove. The Oak Shrine is a holy place of the Woodland God Jykee. It was here that Jykee surrendered to Mipinus ending a long ago war between those gods.”

“Who sent word and how could they have known of us or our purpose?” said Heela.

“All will be revealed in time, come with me now,” said the aged druid.

Gerojef led them to the far side of the grove. An ancient

oak garlanded with dead flowers and unrecognizable debris stood imposing its shadow on the smaller trees surrounding it. Before the tree knelt initiate monks dressed in the same drab brown garb as Gerojef. They turned to look blankly as the party approached. Gerojef motioned them away and they scurried out of the way and exited the grove.

The oak tree was thick; it would have taken two grown men with longish arms to encircle the girth of the giant oak's trunk. It was covered by a dark gray bark, almost black in the shade of the heavily laden branches. As they drew nearer they could see that the underside of the leaves turned from a shiny black-green to a golden brown felt. The ground beneath was strewn with acorns the same size and shape as a child's finger.

Dappled sunbeams revealed a figure stirring at the base of the oak. Woken by their voices as they approached, the figure began to rise, revealing the general outline of a man covered in leaf, vine and clotted earth. The man shape rose slowly, vines seemingly unwrapping themselves from his form and folding back unto the tree. A horn stood out from each side of the man-shape's head and its fur-covered legs ended in hooves. The satyr held a jug in one hand and scratched his groin nonchalantly with the other.

"A goat-man! Scratching himself," said Forenk, first to break the silence.

"Silence child," said Gerojef. He cleared his throat and looked meaningfully at the goat-man. Gerojef spoke to the satyr in the archaic woodland argot.

Gerojef turned back to the Grove's visitors and said, "Before you stands Bahjob and like myself, he is a sworn servitor of Jykee, the Woodland God and Keeper of the Squirrel Sword. He is a child of the wood and vine and in debt to Mipinus."

Bahjob smiling handsomely and spoke-squawked with a voice remarkably similar to the sounds a stomach makes when attempting to digest something indigestible.

Gerojef stoked his long beard and laughed loudly at something Bahjob said but straightened up when everyone turned to stare at him.

"OKAY, that's enough," said Heela with a steely voice that made Forenk start. "Where is this sword?"

The satyr hopped-ran around the bole of the tree, dug at the ground there and returned bearing what looked like a moldy tree limb with a handle. As he handed it gingerly to Heela, she saw that the sword was in a corroded and decaying sheath.

The forest goat-man meanwhile seemed to notice Heela and Donoxa as if waking from a drunken sleep and his features spread into a diabolical leer.

Heela examined the sword but could not determine if the hilt was shaped in the likeness of acorn-capped pillar or in mimicry of the male member. She held the sword at arms length to consider which it was when Bahjob stepped in front of her.

She became aware of a shape similar to the one on the sword's tang growing out of the faun's pubic fur, though his was considerably larger.

"Oh my!" Donoxa said in admiration. The horny satyr responded by leaping upon Donoxa and with an astonishing display of agility, threw her gown up around her neck as they wrestled on the ground rolling, humping, groaning, moaning and grunting, a ball of furry rump and upraised legs. Gerojef gestured at the barbaric effrontery and said, "Be careful, he bites!"

~"~

Meanwhile, Forenk, observing all, turned at the sound of a squeaky scolding from the sacred oak tree just in time to notice a blur of flurried fur flying at him as if shot from a bow. A whirlwind of teeth and claws the size of a large chipmunk's landed on his chest. Forenk slapped, swatted and scratched ineffectually at the minute monster mauling him.

The savage squirrel scampered over Forenk's head and down his lower back to sink his ferocious feral fangs in a frenzy of fury into Forenk's left buttock. Saber teeth, capable of crushing hard nuts in a single nibble ripped through pig-

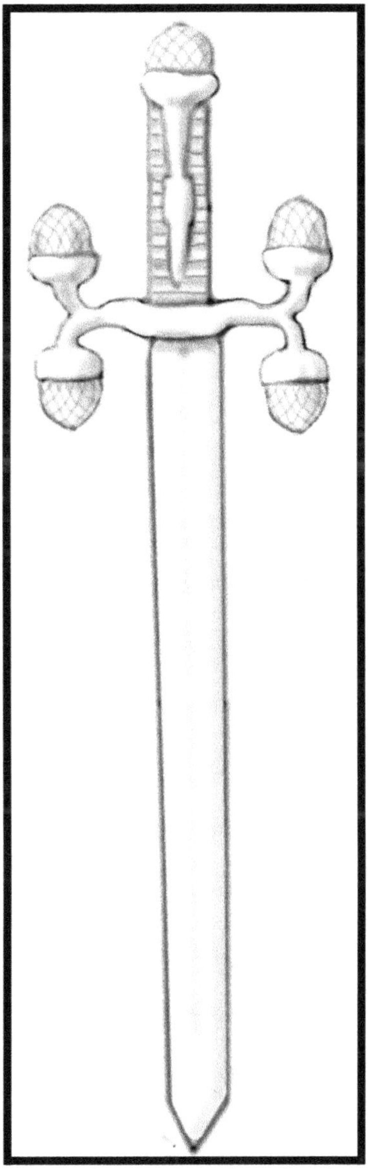

The Squirrel Sword

skin breeks and into the soft tissue and muscle of Forenk's hindquarter. His scream of anguished horror temporarily deafened those nearby and caused wildlife for better than a league away to freeze in fright.

Gerojef responded quickly by adding to the general chaos, holding his open hands skyward he muttered loudly in yet another esoteric language. Heela, in one smooth and purposeful movement unsheathed the Squirrel Sword, stepped behind the bawling and hysterical Forenk and his atavistic appendage, and swung the weapon. A fluffy tail whirled weightlessly for a moment before settling to the ground. The arboreal horror squeaked in dismay and hastily retreated disappearing into the foliage. And as if prior arrangement had been made to stop all activity simultaneously, Donoxa and the faun yodeled in climax as Gerojef ended his paean.

Gerojef walked to where the squirrel tail had fallen. His face grew ashen as if grief stricken. He picked up the tail and examined it thoughtfully. He turned to the others and said, "Dire omens indeed. I am uncertain why the Ancestor Squirrel has attacked you. It has broken the holy covenant of the gods." He looked at the humiliated Forenk, who was busy rubbing his left hindquarter and trying to rein in his blubbering.

Gerojef said, "My mind staggers at the implications of this deed. The power of this grove is destroyed. He watched as leaves started floating to the ground from the sacred oak as if to drive home the point. "My ministrations of this woodland shrine are ended. I will officiate no longer, the Ancestor Squirrel has acted on its own, the sword goes a questing, I find myself at a loss for direction and solace."

"But not for words," said Heela.

Fury burned in Gerojef's eyes for just a moment before he remembered Heela's deft sword swipe and the severed tail in his hand. Instead, he said, "I think it only fitting that you, having created this talisman, should be the one who bears it." He offered the squirrel tail to Heela, who tucked it into her belt.

"Furthermore, said Gerojef, having regained his officious bearings, "We will proceed to the oracle-priest Hezfytis, who sent word of your coming, for ritual cleansing, secret rites and a rede to interpret the actions occurring here, for surely they are prophetic and dire, and signal no small portent."

"Gerojef," said Forenk, who interrupted hesitantly, "I was given a rede by the Goddess Mormoomi."

The Druid did not look surprised or particularly impressed, instead he held his hands aloft and crying out he said, "Mormoomi, the daughter of Simori, Mother of all Rivers, and Tahleos, he who is Father Fate and kens the destiny of all. Laudation to the great gods who rule this world."

Gerojef stopped his panegyric and turned back to Forenk and said, "Yes, she seems to give many divinations, what did your sooth say?"

Forenk repeated Mormoomi's words, trying to mimic the eerie reverberations of her voice. The druid winced as if in pain and Heela stopped Forenk halfway through, recommending that his natural voice might suffice for mortal-to-mortal communication. Forenk repeated the poem of portent to Gerojef.

Look to the goddess of pigs for a sign
Sword of the squirrel bring home to the swine

Heela proposed that the last line clearly suggested returning to Pigland, but Gerojef challenged her assumption, he said, "Ahh, you see, the oracle resides deep in a cave of a mountain, that mountain's name is," he waited for dramatic affect then said "Swine Mountain!"

Gerojef's eyes shone at the mystical coincidence. He said, "I will prepare for our journey at once, for we must have provisions to travel to Swine Mountain, a journey through lands both perilous and fair!"

"Do you mean dangerous and beautiful?" Heela said hopefully, absentmindedly twirling the sword with one hand.

Gerojef watched the graceful display of dexterity for a moment in mild alarm before answering. He said, "No. I meant vermin infested and average."

24 Hegira Resumed

Joined by new traveling companions, the semi-determined team followed a game trail northwest along the river, collecting wild growing fruit and nuts en route. They strode alongside wheat-colored rushes that grew taller than Gerojef and past occasional flowering lianas clinging to half-submerged trees. They crossed rocky streams of rushing water that fed the Nose River.

A multitude of avian chirps, whistles and calls greeted or warned them away from hidden nests. Annoying furry fauna berated them for trespassing into their private territory. There were moments when the river vista reminded Forenk of home and the head waters of the Sty River, where he had first bumped into the girls. Lacking any real ability at imagination he almost pictured his mother and father and the small pig farm where he had spent all but the last few weeks of his life. He tried to remember something else, besides all the misfortune, but had no other memories to recollect.

Then unbidden, words his mother had spoken to him when he was very young, now hauntingly sentimental, repeated themselves in his mind's ear. Mojka had said to him, "Forenk, do not pick your nose in public just because the rest of the village boys do it!" But then she had said something else, something that was starting to make sense. Mojka had said, "For some folk, those of us who are not gods and cannot re-manifest in countless incarnations, life is short. Now mind me, you will do a little better than most, being my son and all, not your average mortal by a long shot."

Forenk had asked his mother, "Will I be able to fly?"

He recalled the look of disappointment in his mother's eyes as she patted him on the head, smiled, and said, "Sure you will, now be a good lad and go practice with your pig poop pusher."

At midday, after a half-day's march, the group of

travelers rested on the bank of the slow moving river and watched as dark clouds rolled in from the South. Bahjob the goat man seemed distracted by something in the woods nearby and leap into the bush. There were sounds of a brief scuffle and Bahjob returned with a large apparently dead snake slung over his sinewy shoulder. Bahjob, speaking in the woodland language no one but Gerojef understood, held the serpent by the tail end showing it to the party. He then stuffed the serpent into a bundle he carried.

Gerojef ordered the group to move on. He said, “We must make use of the day. We will not be able to find our way along in this dense brush this evening because it will be overcast.”

So they rose and renewed the slow paced trek to Swine Mountain. Eventually the river veered off to the West and the barely fervid fellowship continued north. Stopping just before darkness fell, they gathered firewood and prepared to dine on the day’s gathering of edibles. Bahjob produced some berries and the snake he had slain earlier in the day from his travel sack.

He spitted the snake on a stick and then roasted it over the campfire. He held the shish-kebabed serpent with one hand while balancing berries on his nose, letting them roll into his great mouth and devouring them with a few animal-like gulps. Donoxa found amusement in Bahjob’s antics, applauding and urging him on.

Forenk sat quietly by himself trying to chew through a root that seemed tougher than dried pig hide. He listened to Heela as her persistent interrogation of Gerojef continued.

Heela said to Gerojef, “Who is this Oracle of Swine Mountain you speak of and how has he the power of a clairvoyant?”

25 Boring into the Background

Gerojef said, "Hezfytis the Seer was once a distinguished hero of the Gods War. Long ago, in time out of mind, he sustained injuries that would have destroyed lesser men, but he thrives and leads the order of oracles at Swine Mountain."

"That war was a millennia ago, how could this seer, Hezfytis, still live? He would have to be a god himself, is it not so?" she said as she spit a fruit pit into the campfire. The pit crashed into a red burning log that caused a shower of sparks to burst outwards and burn brightly against the blackness surrounding them and cast shadows and light on the attentive figures of the listeners.

The quiet of the night and the crackling of the campfire filled in the silence while Gerojef accepted a section of roasted snake from Bahjob. Before he finished chewing down the serpentine flesh, Heela interrupted him, repeating her question. She said, "How is it that Hezfytis, this hero of the God's War is able to exist so much longer than the mortal span of years?"

Gerojef wiped his greasy hands on his robe and thought about admonishing Heela for her inconsiderate distractions but thought better of it and answered her question. He said, "There was not such a great division between men and immortals in that heroic era. Hezfytis is most likely semi-divine himself."

"His being fey, being able to see into the future, you have witnessed this yourself?" said Heela.

Gerojef said, "His visionary power? Yes, he can predetermine a certain spectra of future events. For instance, he sent word to me of Forenk coming to the sacred grove for the sword."

Heela acknowledged the point with a nod but said, "Do you have a theory as to why the squirrel attacked Forenk? Was it guarding the sword?"

Forenk sat up erect at this and looked at Gerojef expectantly for the answer to the questions.

Gerojef said, “The Sacred Oak, that I have tended for more years than I remember and that has so recently demised, was blessed by the spirit of the Woodland God, Jykee. Jykee is also the Squirrel God and all squirrels own allegiance to him and perhaps to his kith. The squirrel that attacked Forenk possessed a spirit ancestor squirrel, one of the first squirrels of our world.”

“The sword was forged ages ago by the Smith-Priests of the Golden Fire and bound with high magic wards and divine spells. Jykee carried the sword into battle against the Mud God, Mipinus, and surrendered its use unto him when defeated. The ancestor squirrel may have acted to protect the sword although bound to release it when I, the Guardian of the Sacred Grove, passed it on to fulfill Jykee’s oath. Why the squirrel did not act in accordance with the oath, well that is a mystery to me as well.”

“Mipinus?” Forenk asked.

Heela and Donoxa exchanged mischievous glances and then Heela turned to Forenk smiling. She said to him, “Mipinus is the God of Mud, among other things.”

Gerojef said, “And a fertility god and according to the locals, the creator of all men,” and then hastily adding, he said, “and women.” He studied the glow in Heela and Donoxa’s eyes.

“I’m afraid that leads to another question, kindly Gerojef.” said Heela, “Please tell Forenk why the two gods did battle?”

Gerojef said, When the world was young, gods were plentiful. The reason for the battle was that Mipinus, the God of Mud and Fertility, came to these lands and created men from mud. The last, least and lowest form of men in the world to be made are the people of Pigland.”

Gerojef in deference to Forenk and his protectors quickly added, “Or so I have heard.” When he sure there would be no repercussions aside from a slight glare from Heela, he continued his tale.

“Of course, I am not from around here!” Realizing he was making matters worse, Gerojef’s expression changed to that of someone caught molesting a small mammal. He cleared his throat loudly and continuing, said, “The Woodland God, Jykee had ruled the woodlands here for an age before Mipinus and made men out of mud. Jykee protested the invasion, claiming these lands as his own and organized his army of squirrels and other forest beasts, and into the fray went they. But Mipinus’ army of men defeated Jykee’s army of woodland beasts.”

“Mipinus had the power to destroy Jykee’s spirit. Jykee was forced to make an oath of allegiance to Mipinus. The Squirrel Sword of Jykee was sworn to the service Mipinus or his kind if ever the need arose.”

“The Squirrel Sword was placed in the Sacred Grove, lo, countless seasons ago and ever since then hast a druid like myself ministered the grove and over-watched the tree and sword. Men have dominated these lands since that oath binding and up till now the sword has never been sought out.”

Heela said, That does not explain why Forenk was the object of squirrel’s wrath.”

“Aye, as I said, that is a mystery, the Ancestor Squirrel is under the vow of Jykee to aid the seeker of the sword. It would normally act in the best interest and intentions of Jykee. I would have expected its assistance not its hinderance. Perhaps Hezfytis the seer will shed light on the mystery question, when we have audience with him.”

“You have no opinion?” said Heela.

“The Squirrel is not an ordinary squirrel. It is possessed by an ancient ancestor squirrel, one of the first of its kind. Its motive for attacking our friend Forenk could be a matter of personal revenge for the humiliation of Jykee. It is unclear to me. But again, mayhap Hezfytis will be able to elucidate.”

Gerojef got to his feet, produced a coarse blanket from his pack and prepared a bower under the bole of a tree near the fire. He said, “Now, it is time for us to rest, we start off early on the morrow. Good dreams to you fair Heela.”

Heela obligingly wished the druid a good night’s rest then followed his example. Forenk also wrapped himself in his blanket. Donoxa and the goat man had withdrawn discreetly some distance from the diminishing campfire light during the discourse and eventually the grunting and moaning sounds they made subsided into contented sighs and the camp settled down into a sleepy silence.

Forenk, still awake when the others fell into sleep realized that he had not imitated the beasts in the devil's own fornication with the strange young women since they had met up with Black Thumb. Not sure of what to make of that, he decided to put it out of mind and sleep.

However, just as he was dozing off, he spotted a pair of close-set eyes in the shadowy branches above him. The eyes burned with a palpable vehemence that caused Forenk to shiver in terror, prepared to scream. It must have been hours before those tiny dots of dread blinked out and Forenk was able to seek rest. He did not sleep well, even then, nor would he in the nights to come.

26 The Plop Thickens

The group continued north the next morning. As they marched on the river forest melted away into a scrubby plain broken here and there by a copse of trees or a lonely outcrop of rock. In the distance, brownish-gray hills rose to the horizon.

Forenk, exhausted from lack of sleep, stumbled on, feeling raw and as though he were being tested. The land ahead held little sign of life or color. Not a bird or insect could be seen or heard. They passed a lone gnarled tree stripped bare of leaves, it's curling bark the color of fresh ash. Even the sky was shorn of color, a featureless layer of gray cloud cover overcast the world and blocked the sun.

The grim tableau caused Forenk's mind to ponder and wander to the subject of death. As he dragged his feet along bone weary from last night's sleeplessness, he remembered Gerojef's tales of the night before. What kind of world is this, he asked himself. Were events marked and measured by the atrocities of war? Why did horrors, like the squirrel demon that dogged his tracks, exist?

Even as Forenk recalled the dreadful experience with the squirrel he had the feeling of being watched. He turned to look back along the path they walked and saw something small and furry leap behind a small furry bush at the range of his vision.

Alarmed, Forenk walked on scanning the forsaken landscape for signs of the enemy squirrel. He did not see any more of the furtive shape and as ominous as the surroundings were, the dismal day passed uneventfully.

An hour short of sunset the party stopped to make camp. While gathering firewood Gerojef discovered an unattractive herb near one of the twisted and colorless trees that dotted the eerie landscape.

"Ah, I believe this is the rare herb ghost bane," Gerojef said, holding up a pinkish tuber-shaped plant in the fading light. It produces a most useful balm when prepared by boiling it to sludge. "It is a good for communication with the spirit world and keeping hungry ghosts away as it can burn them like fire will to living mortals. Yes, indeed, I shall concoct a salve this very night, it may prove useful."

In a frightened child's voice, Forenk said, "Are there ghosts?" He looked around with wide eyes and said, "Around here?"

Gerojef chuckled and said, "There are ghosts almost everywhere!"

"Why would that be?" said Forenk, his eyes bobbing back and forth in an attempt to pierce the growing gloom.

"Oh, there are many reasons for a spirit to delay its journey to the lands of the dead. Usually some deed that needs to be undone, for instance seeking revenge for a murderer." said Gerojef.

Instantly, the imagined faces of all those who had met their fate as a result of his improbable clumsiness popped up before Forenk.

Gerojef said, "Could be a curse, an unfulfilled quest, the purposes vary. The specter could be commanded by the powers that be to guard an area on which it has committed a breach of loyalty or faith."

"The powers that be?"

"The spirits of gods and demons who rule their own kingdoms in the realms of the dead,"

"Can they harm us?"

"Oh, most certainly," Gerojef said, answering the question almost jovially. "Ghosts are capable of draining your life energy, leaving you a dry crumbling husk. I have seen the end result on more occasions than I care to think about. They can drink blood too, although it has to be spilt as a sacrifice, or when they possess a body and become vampires."
Gerojef stopped his narrative to look in the air before him with an expression of resigned fatalism. He said, "I have heard it is excruciatingly painful as well. If you do not die from the shock and horror of being consumed from beyond the grave first." He sat watching Forenk, smiling at the the reaction his story telling

was having.

Cold chills pounded in the base of Forenk's skull, his dread of the unknown rekindled by Gerojef's explanation of ghosts. With great effort he managed to coax himself back to self-control by reminding himself of his near familiarity with the gods. After all, he was on a first name basis with at least one major deity. Why worry about some lowly spirit stuck clinging to the mundane plane because of some likely moral indiscretion.

After stopping for the day and making camp, the group of travelers prepared and ate a meal while the last few shreds of light from the horizon faded into the pitch-blackness of an overcast evening. The campfire danced, flinging spooky lights that illuminated the faces of the companions into fearful masks, and cast long wicked shadows behind them.

Gerojef finished his meal and sat over his concoction of the herb he had collected earlier, stirring the thickening liquid in a small iron cooking pot he carried for such occasions. He babbled all the while in some incomprehensible mystical language. When he was done boiling the sauce down to sludge, he set it aside to cool.

Shortly after he scooped up the resultant sap into hands and smeared it all over his body, discreetly turning from the girls as he applied it to his chest neck, legs and groin, where he spent an inordinate amount of time.

"Its good for the skin as well!" said Gerojef. He offered the rancid goop to the others, but no one accepted.

"Now, we must first conduct a ritual to call on the dead spirits, they are fond of drinking fresh blood as I mentioned and I will need someone to sacrifice a bit of blood." Gerojef looked around at the party, and said, "Any volunteers?"

Three loud and unhesitant negatives and a goatish bleep startled the druid. Gerojef regained his composure and said, "Very well then, I shall choose a volunteer. Bahjob, I need a bit of blood and you are my chosen initiate, come here and hold out your arm!"

Bahjob shyly hobbled over to the Druid with his head

bowed and a look of skepticism on his suddenly pouty face. Gerojef incised a small scratch on the hairy arm that caused the faun to bleep in what the others imagined to be faun profanity. A few drops of blood trickled into a small wooded bowl the druid held beneath the squirming satyr's arm.

Gerojef in a great show of authority slowly raised the bowl up to the sky. The clouds mysteriously withdrew, revealing two of the three moons. The white and green orbs shone down through wispy veils of cloud cover while Gerojef, druid of the Sacred Oak and Guardian of the Squirrel Sword, blustered an incantation.

The rest of the party waited in suspense and watched curiosity when Gerojef stopped the orison to scratch his face. They waited some more. The litany was voiced several times by Gerojef whose scratching became more noticeable.

Donoxa, who had up until this time, and from the moment she had met Bahjob, been serenely going about in a dreamy satisfied state and whose verbal activity had been limited to passionate moaning and sighs of contentment, started coming to and paying attention. Now it was she and not Heela who interrupted Gerojef.

Donoxa said, "Excuse me, Gerojef, but I have some knowledge of herbs and I do not recall ghost bane requiring a spell being cast. I thought it merely needed to be rubbed into the skin and that alone allowed the subject to be able to communicate with the dead."

Gerojef jerked defensively. He said, "That is true, the magic nostrum requires no speech, I just thought it lent a certain air." He scratched at his arms, face and everywhere the ghost bane agent had been smeared.

Donoxa studied him for a long moment and then said, "Are you aware of blahtwort, a pinkish tuber-shaped plant sharing a remarkable similarity of appearance with ghost bane?"

Gerojef, twitching spasmodically, said, "No, he replied, I am not familiar with blahtwort." The confidence ebbed out of his voice.

"Its properties, when prepared by boiling it to sludge, produce a unguent which causes extreme itchiness and diarrhea," said Donoxa.

Gerojef heard her last words over his shoulder as he ran into the night. The clouds above seemed to concur by hiding the moons behind their darkness and sending a cold rain falling upon the campers.

~"~

In the hours before dawn Forenk dreamed of floods and swimming madly to escape a sea full of murderous squirrels. He emerged from encumbered slumber haggard and soaked with sweat to find Gerojef slinking back to the campsite. The druid had spent the night repeatedly running far enough from the others so as to not disturb them while emptying his bowels onto an undeserving spot of soil that would never harbor life again.

Gerojef, muttering mostly to himself, said, "If the rain had not washed off that blasted and useless sap, I did not get a moments rest, my robe is filthy. I think I sat on an animal out there."

Gerojef continued his tirade as the rest of the camp stirred awake. When Donoxa rose sleepily from where she lay Forenk happened to glance in her direction and noticed something peculiar.

27 Of Flowers and Songs

Flowers of all shapes and sizes surrounded Donoxa's bower, completely incongruous with the sparse and spindly vegetation that survived in the barren prairie they had been traversing the last few days. Every color and variety of fragrant petal and stem spread like a carpet around her drab blanket cloak.

Bahjob pointed to the minute oasis of flowers and exclaimed something in jibber jabber that sounded approving. Forenk looked on in wonder, as did Gerojef, to a lessor extent.

Donoxa smiled as she collected several of the perfumed blossoms into a bouquet and proceeded to weave a garland. When she was finished she placed the sweet smelling chaplet on the crown of her head where it graced her head and gave her the semblance of a queen of nature.

Heela unsurprised by the miraculous appearance of a garden springing up while they were sleeping sharpened the blade edges of the Squirrel Sword on a suitable stone.

Gerojef finally broke the silence of the magical tableau by saying to Donoxa, "I suspected from the first, you and Heela are divinities of some kind, angelic nymphs here to guide Forenk on his quest."

"I knew it!" blurted out Forenk, the excitement of realization animating his normally bland expression.

Heela hesitated for a moment, smiling pleasantly, she resumed grinding the edge of the Squirrel Sword without saying anything.

Donoxa said, "Forenk's destiny remains to be determined. We follow and aid Forenk until he discovers his purpose. Most mysteries are divulged in time. I think the Oracle at Swine Mountain may cast some illumination on the path that lies in darkness."

Heela looked up and said, "We have made little effort to hide our purpose. We are not exactly what you say we are,

Gerojef, but neither are we not."

Donoxa turned to Forenk and said, "The gods take interest in your existence and we are here to guide you as we can, dear boy. Remember there was a curse placed upon you from birth. Donoxa has passed the bad luck hex on to Black Thumb, who demonstrated to us that he sorely deserved it. We can thank the Captain for that, for I would not have been able to remove it unless I had a suitable host. We would not want to place a curse like that on an innocent."

Heela said, "But we must remember, someone very powerful put that curse on you."

Donoxa said, "I could not dispel the curse it, it was so strong that I could only move it."

Forenk nodded and said, "Was pretending to enjoy fornication with scores of salty sailors for my benefit?"

The two young angelic women laughed like inebriated pixies, "No, we did that for fun. We are representatives of Mipinus, and he is the the God of Fertility, after all!"

Gerojef proposed that they move on and so they gathered up the few belongings and began to head up the trail. Donoxa wreathed in flowers in a wasteland devoid of color.

The girls marched along and soon began humming.

As they wended their way along, the scrubby desolation gave way to greenery, bright grass and taller healthy-looking trees swaying in a mild breeze. Birds and bees chirped and buzzed in cadence with the singing as the hills moved closer. In that moment it seemed to Forenk that the world was magical and a feeling of joy expanded from that sense of wonder to over come his bone weariness. He practically skipped along and without consciously deciding to do so and found himself calling out a verse to the tune the girls hummed.

Yes, the road has been a rough one
Many evils have assailed my skin
But from now we progress uphill
From this moment I begin...

All were relieved to be interrupted by Bahjob calling out satyr gibberish from a distance ahead where he had been scouting. He pointed to the ground where he stood.

"What did Bahjob say?" Forenk said Gerojef, wondering if it would be okay to continue singing.

Gerojef hurried his pace and without looking back, said "He said you might want to hold off on the singing and come look!"

They all trotted over and when they got there Bahjob pointed to what they could now see was a depression in a muddy spot. The depression clearly resembled a very large cloven hoof.

Heela and Gerojef decided what ever it was, it was bipedal, walking on two legs.

"Demon," said Heela.

"Big demon," added Gerojef.

The squirrel automatically popped up in Forenk's mind. He had not seen it last night or today.

Somehow, he imagined, it had transformed into a giant monster and would soon devour him and his benefactors. Donoxa had told him that not all the gods favored him. It only took one annoyed or even slightly displeased god to make one's life extremely unpleasant. Confused, Forenk worried guiltily. What had he done to find himself surrounded by fanged and drooling monsters who seemed to be lining up to get snapping fangs into him.

"It is the squirrel, he has been turned into a giant monster by one of those gods who does not like me!" Forenk fairly squealed out loud, thinking to himself that at least that would mean only one unholy monster instead of two.

Gerojef said, "Rest easy Forenk, even a giant squirrel would not have hoofs. Although they would tend to have huge claws capable of easily disemboweling their enemies." He looked pointedly at Forenk and said, "My guess would be some monstrous demon from a lower level of the chaos hells summoned by a foul and malevolent enemy of yours."

"That is not comforting at all," said Heela. "I think I

prefer the squirrel theory!"

Bahjob stood facing the rest of the party and spoke with great emphasis, asking a question in his unintelligible goat-man argot.

"What did he say now? said Heela to Gerojef.

"He has posed a riddle of some sort. He asked what is twice the height of a man, has two heads, giant tentacles and pincer claws filled with spikes the length of swords and drips green smoking venom."

"Thats a strange riddle," said Forenk.

"I will ask him what the answer to the riddle is," said Gerojef. He asked Bahjob for the answer to the riddle in the woodland tongue and turned back to Forenk and the girls, his face turning ashen as he said, "Bahjob Said he did not know either but it's coming up behind us."

28 Of Demonic Monsters from the Pits of Hell

They all turned slowly, taking a moment to glance at each other, acknowledging that this was one of the unexpected sequences of the quest that they would have been unwilling to have roles in if there were a choice to be made.

Before them at not very far a distance approached a demon. It was twice the height of a man. It did indeed, as Bahjob had pointed out, have two heads, tentacles and crab-like claws filled with spikes the length of swords that were dripping green smoking venom. Its bulbous rounded pair of heads were covered by long brownish-gray fur and where eye sockets should have been, long curving horns protruded and swept backwards out of its skull.

The demon had been moving at a stealthy pace suited for sneaking up on its prey, and even without eyes, it reacted to their attention. The demon bellowed a sound, not often heard in the mortal world, then lowered its mammoth woolly head and charged.

It is said that an immediate and perilous event can cause a participant in that event to perceive time as proceeding in slow motion, and in some instances, where loved ones are threatened for instance, the said participant gains extraordinary strength and prowess. Forenk, on the other hand, felt faint and the world sped up into a frenzied whirlwind as the grotesque demonoid bore down on them with supernatural agility. Forenk would have made a half heated attempt at bravery but a distressingly familiar movement from a nearby tree caught his eye.

Even as the giant demonic terror loomed towards him, Forenk turned towards the tree revealing the nightmare squirrel preparing to leap to the attack. Forenk's bowels froze and his face contorted into a mask of agonized fright as the tailless figure leapt from the limb it was perched on.

Forenk reacted quickly. He stumbled backwards and

Demon Attack

tripped over his own feet. He landed on the rocky ground with a bone-jarring thud. The squeaking menace pounced on Forenk's supine form and deftly burrowed into his pigskin trousers. Hysterically Forenk sought an action that might stop this untoward invasion of his underwear, but fearing the consequences of angering an already vicious mammal lodged in his pants, he did nothing as it burrowed to his crotch. His eyes widened in realization of what was happening as the squirrel bit in.

Heela had the Squirrel Sword out of her belt and in hand the moment she faced the demon monster. Calculating the powers of the hell-sent agent before her, she advanced purposely as it charged.

Gerojef overcame the primal terror turning his knees to jelly, he raised his staff above his head and remonstrated to any nature god that might be inclined to listen to his spell plea.

Donoxa tore the flowered garland from her head and flung it at the unholy beast as she swore in an arcane tongue. The air rippled before her as she sang the song spell. The flowers in the garland unwound themselves and transformed into butterflies, the colorful petals each turned into a colorful butterfly with wings of the flowers color. A hundred butterflies fluttered and swooped in loose formation directly in to the path of the grotesque behemoth. Distracted momentarily, the hell-beast swung tentacles and snapped giant claws ineffectually at the rippling mass that swirled around it.

Heela moved in close and swung the sword with great precision at one of the thick snake limbs. The cleanly severed serpentine tentacle gushed green steaming fluid as it fell and then squirmed on the ground. The devilish creature moaned low and turned its attention from the butterflies to Heela. She dodged the lunge of a massive pincer claw, ducking low and rolling to the side. Heela came up swinging the sword and sheared away half a giant claw.

The monster bellowed and the remaining section of claw sprayed greenish ichor in a wide arc. Caught off guard by the demon's spasm-like reaction, the opposite claw smashed into

Heela like a club the size of a tree trunk. As she flew through the air and blackness descended on her, she heard Forenk's shrieking scream intermingled chaotically with spell song, druid's prayer and demon roar.

The battalion of butterflies danced around the demon as it swung its remaining appendages ineffectually. The monster issued an ear-piercing howl as a large rock thrown by Bahjob cracked into the one of the foul heads. Bahjob nimbly hurled another melon-sized stone at the monster's injured head and one of its eye-horns splintered. The demon detected Bahjob and charged, leaving a trail of green foam globules in its wake.

Bahjob was caught off balance as he hefted a two-handed rock to bash the enraged demon. The demon's tentacles wrapped Bahjob in whipping coils and jerked him towards the horrible creature's remaining poisoned claw. The stone dropped harmlessly to the ground as the venomed spikes in the pincer claws pierced Bahjob's body. For a moment he twisted and writhed madly but his skin turned gray, first from where the spikes pierced his flesh and then spread upward and out. Bahjob's struggles slowed and he hung limply impaled on the spikes. The colossal beast shook Bahjob's inert body from its claw and turned to face those remaining.

Donoxa and Gerojef cast their magic spells frantically. Donoxa focused on casting a new spell and the magic that had changed the flowers to butterflies wore off. The fragile pastel petals gently settled to the ground, contrasting vividly with the smoking green goo the gruesome monstrosity was bleeding and the gore of what once was Bahjob. The monster demon had no face, certainly no observable mouth but despite its heavy wounds and severed appendages it seemed to grin as it lumbered the short distance to it's remaining prey.

Before it could reach Donoxa and Gerojef, tree roots like living serpents erupted from the ground before the behemoth demon. The woody snakes grasped and twined around the demon's legs, it's remaining tentacle and claw squabbled and wrestled with the wooden foe.

Gerojef had called upon the living tree spirits for aid

and his prayer-spell had been answered. He collapsed to the ground exhausted from the effort just as Donoxa's divine magic took shape. Blue fire played along her arms and leapt from her hands to the monster's head where it ignited the furry covering. The grating bellow that issued from the beast drowned out Forenk's pitiful squealing moans. Donoxa chanced a look in his direction.

Forenk, his trousers around his ankles, was on his knees shaking as he held something on the ground. Then Donoxa turned back to see the demon breaking loose of the snake-like tree roots, its head wreathed in blue flame, its roar deafening as it took one lumbering step towards her. Somehow it stood for a moment on one leg, the other still held by the tree roots. Then the huge demon fell to the ground. Heela stood behind him, bruised and bloody, the sword slimy with green gore. She had chopped through one giant leg with the vorpal blade of the Squirrel Sword. The massive form of the demon shivered a few times as it burned and disintegrated. The putrid stench of burning demon flesh filled everyone's nostrils as the tail-less ancestor squirrel, something in its mouth, scampered away chittering.

29 Sorting out the Sordid Stuff

"I thought you said this place was not dangerous!" said Heela to Gerojef. The blood that ran down her forehead emphasized her words. Gerojef dusted himself off without bothering to reply.

"The squirrel bit off one of my wobblies!" cried Forenk. Donoxa turned to him alarmed, and said, "Oh, this bodes ill, your wobblies hold the last of the divine seed in all of Pigland. We must put an end to that vengeful squirrel before it destroys the heritage of Mipinus."

Donoxa's meanwhile stood over the remains of Bahjob. She said, "My poor Bahjob, he died trying to protect us." A teardrop rolled slowly down her perfect cheek.

"He was a little wild, but a faithful companion," said Gerojef. He sniffled and said, "Surely we will all miss him."

Forenk tried to observe the moment's solemnity but could not help moaning in pain. He said, "I am sorry for Bahjob, but by the gods, it hurts." Forenk started to croak something else but passed out.

After collecting nearby herbs Gerojef and Donoxa mixed the ingredients. They cleaned the wounds and Donoxa stitched up the wounds with healing magic. They applied the poultice made from the herbs to Forenk and Heela's wounds and wrapped them in bandages improvised from leaf, vine and torn cloth. Bahjob was laid to rest at the base of one of the rare healthy looking trees in the area. Gerojef recited a farewell to his brave servant.

~"~

Forenk regained consciousness as the battle-weary group settled in for the night and asked if the bad luck curse were truly gone, thinking back upon his stumbling fall during the attack.

"Yes, I am certain the curse is gone," said Donoxa.

"Your just very clumsy," said Gerojef, "and you may want to keep an eye out for any strange growths or changes in his anatomy."

"Strange growths?" said Forenk.

"Yes, strange growths or changes in your anatomy, like a tail stump or your front teeth starting to stick out," said Gerojef.

Forenk started to say something but winced in pain from the effort.

"For the sake of Thegotta, why would that happen?" said Heela.

"Well, Forenk has been bitten by the magical ancestor squirrel, it only stands to reason that you may succumb to lycanthropism, he may become a were-squirrel!" Forenk stared in numb horror at Gerojef, whose smug expression resembled an ironic grin made eerie by the reddish campfire light. "Gerojef, do not torment him," Heela said. "He has been through enough today, as we all have." "I merely point out a very plausible possibility," said Gerojef, assuming an innocent and offended tone. "Yes, but you also derive some pleasure from your instruction, do you not?" said Heela.

Gerojef, assuming the pompous stance he used in defense when challenged, apologized with a caveat. He said, "But it is possible, is it not?" He turned to Donoxa.

"It is not impossible," was Donoxa's short but unsure sounding reply.

There was a tense moment in which none spoke but all could feel Forenk's fear through the dark like a cold tingling pressure on their skin.

Deciding no further information was forthcoming and in search of less troubling thoughts, Forenk changed the subject. He said, "Donoxa, you said I carried the last divine seed of Pigland. How can that be? I was born of mortals."

Forenk paused, thought for a moment and then said, "Although my mother was always carrying on about gods and divinity, I assumed she was merely eccentric until I started this adventure with you and Heela." He stared into the firelight and said, "Of course only an idiot and a coward like myself would not see the truth right in front of me, I suppose. If it is the truth, that is."

Gerojef put his arm around Forenk's shoulder like a father who realizes he has been insensitive to his son and said, "I do not think anyone would call you a coward, as for being an idiot, well, you are certainly not a coward."

Donoxa commanded Gerojef to silence with a hand motion and spoke in a calming voice to Forenk. She said, "Ignore Gerojef's words. He has much wisdom and has aided us in our quest, but in matters of relations he is a novice and has much to learn." She stared at Gerojef meaningfully. Gerojef quickly decided this was a good time to remove his sandals and give them a good examination. He held the worn and dusty footwear up in the firelight and eyed them carefully.

"My mother claimed to be a goddess," said Forenk, "and now I see I am involved with Mipinus somehow."

Donoxa's face grew radiant. She smiled and said, "Your mother is the incarnation, the last manifestation of Thegotta, the Pig Goddess. Your father is Mipinus, the God of Mud and Fertility.

A sudden wind blew sparks from the brightly burning fire wood and made a wooing sound.

Donoxa said, "I speak too freely. The wind and the spirits that surround us carry our words to ears that they were not meant for. Perhaps I have said more than is wise."

Heela took Donoxa's hand and faced her. They began to sing again and their voices transformed into a twin tingling timbre. Together they said, "You and Gerojef have guessed or realized the secrets we took no great pains to disguise. For Forenk is the sole progeny of the gods of pigs and fecundity." They laughed and still speaking as one, said, "We will not be allowed to stay here with you on the earthly plane if we divulge too much."

Donoxa spoke on her own, she said, "Divinities must take care when they interfere in mortal lives for fear of disturbing the affairs of other gods. Even the gods must beware the delicate balance of the cosmos. You are unique, and our mission one of importance, but in assisting you we come into conflict with other powers. We give them license to act in response by violating matters in the world of mortals."

Forenk said, "What gods would be observing us, who sent you to protect me, are you goddesses?"

The angelic duo smiled at each other again. Donoxa said, "No, not goddesses, but we are what men might call divine spirits."

Gerojef thought about asking them what women called them but decided better against it. Instead he said, "Divine spirits, I knew it. Angels, sort of. One of magic, one of war."

Heela said, "The divine have many names, but imagine the place where the gods reside as a storm cloud and individual gods manifesting as lightning forms from the cloud. The gods and spirits are everywhere and everything is connected. It is a flux of forces, the gods are in a constant power struggle. Divine spirits, such as ourselves are agents of the mighty entities, and they can cause the manifestation of divine spirits Do you understand?"

Forenk said, "No, not completely, but it sort of makes some sense, I guess." He hesitated for a moment and then said, "I have another question. I am the offspring of this Mud God of Fertility, yet I am mortal. How can that be?"

"Your husk, your body that is, is mortal, as our own bodies are for the time being, but your spirit is descended from the divine. We were sent to be your companions but we know not your fate. You must fulfill some destiny, we follow the trail and wait for the signs as you do. So far we have been led to the temple of Thegotta and Gerojef, who leads us to the oracle of Swine Mountain."

Donoxa picked up the conversation as if she and Heela were the same person speaking. She said, "What we do know of your purpose, Forenk, is that you carry the last seed of the gods of Pigland and beyond. Your offspring will be the last to carry the blood of the gods and to be born of mortal womb."

Forenk nodded with comprehension, much to the surprise of the others. he said, "And the squirrel?"

Heela said, "Perhaps as Gerojef postulated, an enemy of your father seeking vengeance for the humiliation suffered by Jykee, the Woodland and also the god of squirrels."

Forenk said, But Gerojef said Jykee under oath to aid Mipinus."

Gerojef said, "Yes, the squirrel should be under that oath as well, being a subject of Jykee! But for some unknown reason it seems single minded in seeking vengeance on you, Forenk, son of Mipinus and Thegotta. Maybe to stop the birth of Mipinus' descendants, to end the family line."

Discussing the squirrel dismayed Forenk and he moaned out the words, almost crying he said, "The squirrel got away with one of my wobblies!" He tried unsuccessfully to hold back his tears while he said, "Was the big demon helping the squirrel?"

No one offered an opinion but it did seem that the two, the demon goliath and the fanatic squirrel, were working together.

After a long silence, Gerojef said, "It is likely that there is a connection, if what you say is true about Forenk and your purpose here, the squirrel and the demon may only be the beginning of our troubles."

30 To Sleep, Perchance to Scream

The conversation eventually ended and all prepared to retire for the day. After the day's exertions they all quickly faded into deep sleep except for Forenk whose stomach roiled in agitation as he tossed and turned beneath his blanket and unable to doze off because of the unsettling possibility the future held.

Eventually he managed drift into a disturbed slumber but was awoken by a strange sensation around his jaws. He opened his eyes to find a squirrel's snout where his nose should have been. In horror he felt at the hairy protruding muzzle. In panic he mistook something digging into the base of his spine for the turbulence that precedes breaking wind but when it continued and he pulled down his pants and out popped a giant furry squirrel's tail!

Suddenly, the tailless squirrel that had haunted his days and nights appeared before Forenk laughing and pointing at Forenk's new squirrel-like face. Forenk leapt from his blanket screaming, "I've been turned into a were-squirrel, I have a tail and a funny nose! I m cursed for life, I've lost one of my balls and now I look like a squirrel, woe is me!"

"Forenk, you have not changed into a squirrel. You are having a nightmare," said Heela.

Forenk started awake, looked around for the squirrel but saw only the sympathetic faces of Heela and Donoxa and the the somewhat amused Gerojef.

Gerojef said, "Wait, turn around. My word, you do have a tail! Oh, no, that is just your shirttail. Heh, heh, sorry about that, it was hard to tell in the dark. But now that that is sorted out, shall we get back to sleep? We have a long march ahead of us." Gerojef turned and disappeared under his blanket.

"Are you all right Forenk?" said Donoxa.

Forenk nodded and said, "I suppose I am, he said unconvincingly."

His guardians sat with him on a log and threw fresh wood on the fire that had burned down to cinders while they slept. Donoxa threw her arm around Forenk and Heela offered to start instructing him in swordplay the next day and the thought of chopping the damned squirrel in two cheered Forenk up considerably.

"Gerojef was right. We do have a long march ahead of us. Let us off to rest and get an early start on the morrow," said Heela.

They were soon wrapped in their blankets fast asleep except for Forenk who lay awake with his head propped against his pack. Gerojef snored on the other side of the fire. Forenk could not settle down and instead imagined shapes in the darkness and wondered if they should have posted a sentry, someone to watch out in case of attack. It was all very fine to be escorted by such capable companions, but things had gotten too close for comfort with the squirrel bite and that demon. The thought sent shivers up his spine. How could he possibly sleep knowing demons were out to get him?

The squirrel was surely possessed by a demon or some kind of mad spirit and had already gotten a part of Forenk that left an aching void. There was no way he would be able to sleep without a guard posted. So he sat till his eyelids hung heavy and closed of their own accord.

31 Is NightMare-ly for Sleeping

Forenk heard a deliciously sultry voice waking him from within a dream. "Lovely man-boy, favorite of the gods, come to me!" The lovely sound sent warm thrills through his body. He opened his eyes and could see a
woman's radiant shape just beyond the edge of the camp and partially hidden in the trees.

"Who are you?" said Forenk, vaguely aware that the others did not stir although he was nearly yelling. "Come, favored one, come and love me," said the glistening woman in the shadows of the trees. She projected so much attraction that Forenk found himself tossing his blanket aside and rising to stand.

The words of that unbearably sensual feminine speaker made Forenk break into a cold sweat even though the air was cool. His face flushed. He knew there was something wrong, some danger lurked in her speech but the temptation was a wave of power through his body. He thought of Mormoomi and the incredible passion she had unleashed in him. The divinities of the land wanted his children and obliging them was the most pleasure he had ever known.

He walked towards the woman in the shadows of the trees.

She was beautiful even by comparison with Donoxa, Heela, Mormoomi and the sea nymphs. She was truly god-like in form and bearing. Her hair shone like polished bronze and her smile was dazzling, her eyes were like beacons of salvation from a complex confusing world.

Her white delicate garments revealed the ample ravishing form beneath. Her least movement exuded a hot sensuality that made Forenk dizzy with lust. His legs became unsteady and his heart pounded when the few filaments of silky gown slipped over her shoulders and slowly slid over her shapely hips to the ground.

Forenk barely observed or wondered how the night had become so well lit and why everything else in the world seemed to be missing, everything but this woman and her hypnotic beauty. For a moment he thought about asking this dream-like vision her name, that would be the proper thing to do, but instead he undid his belt and dropped his trousers to his ankles. His manhood filled with the blood of passion sprang out and nearly pointed straight up to the sky.

Forenk felt like he had shed the skin of his past and left it behind. The quest was a fine idea but the others would do better without his help anyway. True salvation stood before him. He would follow this singular goddess or what ever she was, wherever she went, no matter what happened next.

Sweat beaded Forenk's forehead and made his pig skin jerkin stick to his skin as she approached but it grew darker suddenly and Forenk could see that he had been deceived.

Instead of a glittering forest nymph, the beauteous goddess he had seen only moments before, a reptilian form with leathery skin stood revealed before him. It was a sickly green in color and covered with hideous lumps and barbed whiskers. A tongue as long as his arm sprang past her pointy teeth. The she-thing's powerful arms were knotted with twitching sinewy muscle.

Forenk cringed and his insides swam with nausea beholding her slimy repugnant visage. The stink of animal filth filled his nostrils as he froze for a moment in terror.

The she-thing laughed in an inhuman voice and said, "Your sword seems to be shrinking." She pointed a long pointed and gnarled finger towards his rapidly dwindling tumescence.

In a mad sound bred in hell she laughed again and said, "If you re not going to be using it, you will not mind if I eat it."

The she-creature leaped for him and her mouth seemed to enlarge like a serpent's. Forenk reacted by trying to run but instantly tripped over his pants. The monster passed over him raking his side with long claws, landed on all fours, and quickly turned to charge again like some tremendous hunting cat. Forenk could see her muscles tense for the leap. He froze

The True Form of the Succubus

in fear as his stomach clenched and imagined what it would be like to have his flesh ripped from his body.

The black fathomless cat eyes of the she-monster widened and glared at Forenk and a voice something like a deep crow's caw spoke, "The smell of fear, how I love that smell! Come, soil yourself, and add to that wonderful perfume."

The she-beast smiled a needle-fanged caricature of a human smile, its whiskers moving like tentacles around its head. "I m going to eat you while you are alive so I can enjoy your screams, you little filth." The horror inched closer and bunched up its muscles to leap.

Forenk closed his eyes, his body tightening up and waited for the inevitable. He felt a sharp slap across his face.

"Awaken, Forenk, awaken!" said Donoxa. Magically he was back at the camp with the others, still in his blanket. Donoxa and Gerojef stood above him. A sparkling residue, like the trail of a magic spell lingered in the air. His side hurt.

"Succubus! A demon that disguises itself as an object of lust in a dream to lure a victim into their clutches," said Gerojef, basing his conjecture on Forenk's description. They had been forced to arouse him by using a waking spell when his terrified moan had woken the others.

"It seems I am not safe in this world or the one of dreams," said Forenk.

"Not so, rest easy Forenk, I will safe guard you from harm while you sleep with my magic. I will cast a dream ward to protect your rest," Donoxa said. She waved her hands, pronounced words that Forenk had never heard before and drew signs in the air that hung like a faint mist.

"Sleep now and rest undisturbed till morning bird doth sing," said Donoxa.

"By the Squirrel Sword, no creature of this world will harm you while I stand sentinel," said Heela.

"And, on the morrow, I will prepare breakfast," said Gerojef with a mild flourish.

32 In the Shadow of Mt Swine

The next day Gerojef prepared the morning meal. River water mixed with the last of the grain he had brought from the sacred grove was cooked to make a thick porridge that they sweetened with honey stolen from a bee's nest. To this they added a wild berries picked along the path.

After they had eaten, Heela said, "As I promised, and if you are for it, Forenk, I will teach you the fundamentals of sword play."

Heela proceeded to cut down a few suitable branches from the nearest large tree. She trimmed them into the general shape of a sword. She then gave Forenk the Squirrel Sword and she herself used the sculpted tree limbs as swords to fence with him. The branches were quickly sliced to stumps by the magical blade.

Heela was a superb instructor and Forenk an apt pupil, so the lesson was very productive. Forenk was determined to learn to defend himself and he entertained fantasies of slicing up the squirrel that he knew lurked somewhere nearby waiting for the right moment to go after his remaining testicle. Even so, he felt surprisingly well rested and pleased that the Squirrel Sword seemed to suit him so well.

"The sword's sacred powers show through when you wield it Forenk. Although it got the job done for me, I felt something asleep in the weapon when I used it," said Heela.

"It does seem to favor me," said Forenk. He smiled as the sword practically twirled itself in his hand.

He searched the nearby trees for a sign of the Ancestor Squirrel and with the Squirrel Sword in his hand the squirrel seemed like little danger.

"We must train you to overcome your shyness and live up to your potential, Forenk. But do not get over confident. That is the worst mistake to be made and will lead to your undoing," said Heela. "A well-balanced sword, no matter how sharp, will be of no avail if you underestimate your enemies."

After the sword practice was concluded, they gathered up what little there was of camp and were on the march again and they soon spied the mountain that was their destination.

Although they had started out late in the morning, Mt. Swine drew near quickly and they found them selves in the shadows at the foot of the mountain before dusk fell.

33 That Gates on My Nerves

The light had all but faded as the travelers reached the fortified entrance to the caverns of the Oracle of Mt. Swine. Torches burned above a large iron-braced wooden door gate built into a fortification barring entrance to the caves beyond. A guard wearing armor over a faded robe and wielding a crossbow, peered down from the low tower of a palisade built above the gate and blocking entrance to where the Oracle dwelt. He eyed them suspiciously and said, "What business have ye at Mt. Swine?"

"You do not have to yell, you are only a few feet away," said Heela.

The guard said, "What was that, could you speak any louder? I am a little hard of hearing?" "Thungi," Gerojef said, addressing the sentry, "It is I, Gerojef, Druid of the Sacred Grove. I have with me the one who bears the, until now dormant and sleeping for ages past, Squirrel Sword. Your master sent for us, let us in to see the Oracle."

Thungi, the guard said, "Gerojef, yes, you look like Gerojef, and you know my name, but…." "But what?" said Gerojef. "You might be up to something. A demon loosed upon the land was spied not far from here. You could be a demon shape shifter disguised as Gerojef. And these young women with you, they are unnaturally alluring. I am having some difficulty remembering my vows of chastity, a sure sign of deviltry," said Thungi.

Gerojef said, "We slew a hideous devil monster and young Forenk here was almost undone by a foul succubus." He gestured to Donoxa and Heela, "These two are the nearest things to angels you will see in your life," Gerojef recalled Donoxa and Bahjob's spirited high jinks, "more or less."

Thungi thought for a moment and said, "I do not know. I would hate to be tricked into being eaten by a foul hell-born demon. What about giving me the passwords?"

The druid turned to his companions and said with only a smidgin of annoying bombast, I must perform the sacred parlance of similarities with the warden of the oracle.

Gerojef turned back to Thungi and said, “The truth is a covert courtesan.”

“The truth is a strange slattern,” said Thungi. “The truth is a bizarre bint,” said Gerojef after a moment’s pause. “The truth is a stubborn strumpet!” said Thungi, almost stuttering.

Gerojef smiled patronizingly and said, “The truth is a testy tart.”

“The truth is a haughty, harlot!” said Thungi.

Gerojef seemed perplexed and pulled at his beard for a long moment and finally said, “The truth is a holoparasitic hussy!”

“The truth is a heretical hetaera,” said Thungi.

“Enough!” said Heela. She gracefully drew the Squirrel Sword from Forenk’s belt and pointed it at Thungi and said, “The truth is, if you do not open the gate, you will have no problem keeping your vows of chastity!”

~”~

Moments later Thungi led the party past the gate and through the roughly carved entrance and into the dark passageways of the caverns. Forenk marveled at the runes and painted images on the walls they walked past. He studied the pictographs of warrior gods and beasts in battle and what looked to him like various rituals or ceremonies based on the what little he knew of them. In one a holy man of some kind held a dagger while blood spilt from the neck of a large beast in another a man tied spread eagle on a painted frame bled from wounds from the many javelins or arrows that pierced his body. Forenk had heard of sacrifices to appease the gods but had never seen art that could communicate complex ideas. So engrossed was he that he had to double step to catch up with the group as they followed Thungi through a musty smelling, mist-filled second corridor to a cavern filled with even more smoke and a sharp stench.

A group of robed attendant monks turned to them and stood at attention as they entered the smoky chamber. Thungi exchanged dialog with the others and sent two of the acolytes to fetch refreshments for the travelers.

"What is that horrible stink?" said Forenk, who was used to working intimately with porcine excrement.

"It is the sacred mist of the Sybil," said one of the attendants.

"Its pretty awful," said Thungi, "I have to get used to it every time I come back in from guard duty."

The attendant monks returned with a tray stacked with food, an amphora of drink and a large bucket to clean up with. "You may nourish yourselves and rest while Hezfytis prepares for you," said Thungi.

The travel-worn group accepted the offered grub. Oblivious to the odor, Forenk, Heela, Donoxa and Gerojef washed off the travelers grime and filled themselves with bread, honey, salted fish, sun-dried fruit and sour tasting wine at a rough-hewn stone table.

As they ate they listened to Thungi and the attendants arguing over who would introduce them to the head of their order, Hezfytis. The attendant monk who won the honor of presenting them to Hezfytis came over when it looked like they were finished eating.

"I will take you to the Oracle now," the monk said. He had a curious smile that made Forenk think that he was in on a joke with the other monks.

34 The Head Oracle

They followed the attendant monk through a doorway opposite the one they had entered. The rest of the monks filed in behind them as they walked down a short corridor that opened into a circular hall. The noxious smell from the last chamber was even stronger and the walls shone with a greenish brilliance although there were no torches or braziers burning.

Gerojef studied the vegetable growth wrapping itself around a crystal-looking material that was the source of the weird green light.

"Is that magic light?" asked Forenk.

Gerojef said, "These are serizine crystals. That moss that grows around the crystals acts like a catalyst and causes the release of that curious glow. It is a natural occurring form of magic."

In the light from the glowing crystals they could see a small pool of what looked like green milk, fed by a spring and draining back into the wall. As they approached the oracular water, nostrils stung and caused faces grimaced, for it was from this pool of bubbling and misty liquid that the acidic-tanged stench that hung throughout the cave complex originated.

Forenk noticed a pedestal positioned in the middle of the room that had what looked like a mummified head resting on it. The attendant walked over to the pedestal, turned to Forenk, and gestured to the object on it without explanation.

Forenk took a closer look and said, "Is that a real head? It looks very old."

The eyes of the head opened and the lips stretched into a broad smile. The head said, "You were expecting a younger man?"

The attendant monk smirked and said, "This is Hezfytis, the hee, hee, Head of the Order of the Oracle of Swine Mountain." The monk tried so hard to hold in his laugh that tears rolled down his face. The other attendants and Thungi,

The Head Oracle

attempting to display some form of solemnity, choked back laughter that sounded like dry heaves and choking.

Hezfytis said, "My servants like to amuse themselves at my expense, and I do not discourage it, I am way a-head of them."

Forenk said, "It is certainly an honor to finally come face to face with you after...."

Forenk was interrupted by the monks laughter echoing back and forth between the chambers of stone.

After a long while and a few more heady puns, wooden stools were brought for the guests who sat in a semi circle facing Hezfytis.

"Gerojef, High Druid Guardian of the Sacred Oak Grove, it has been a very long time since last we spoke," said Hezfytis.

Gerojef said, "That was many a season ago, I recall you had just received news of the Witch Queen of Malborea's victories and there was much war to the North and still is I hear, although here and in Pigland there was mostly quiet."

Several hours later Hezfytis was concluding a tale of someone's past adventures. Concluding the tale, he said, "He was so tough that even while imprisoned for twenty years by the Eastern Emperor he wrote a 16 volume work. I believe it was entitled, 'On being imprisoned for twenty years by the Eastern Emperor.' Yes, well, in any event, he wrote upon paper made from a paste of dried cobwebs, dust balls and saliva pressed into the thinness of paper. For ink he used urine with a feces pigment. While not many have bothered to read his work, it is a testament to human determination and courage and there is a lesson to be learned by all."

Forenk, somewhat out of character, said to Hezfytis, "How do we know you are really thousands of years old?"

"Well," said the head oracle, "the fact that I am a decapitated head should lend some credence to the possibility that I am extraordinary."

Gerojef said, "Ah, it seems that our young Forenk has been transformed from a shallow caricature of simplicity, incapable of original thought, into a curious investigator. Once only capable of the pointlessly expected dialog, he now inquires and even questions. I guess he is not the empty-headed puppet I thought he was. Such an alteration! No rarer deed could provide proof of a greater intelligence guiding us!"

Hezfytis said, "Actually, it is probably the mist of the oracles. It makes my attendants quite impertinent, as you no doubt noticed. I just go along with it, no use beating your head against the wall."

Someone in the next alcove laughed.

Hezfytis said, "See what I mean, it never ends. One has to accept or go mad."

Heela was clearly losing patience but kept quiet. Donoxa said, "Perhaps we could discuss Forenk's fate before we retire. The hour grows late!"

There was a general agreement and Hezfytis was now all seriousness and business. He studied Forenk and scanned the rest of the group before him. Once he was satisfied that everyone paid attention he continued. He said, "I have inhaled the sacred mist of the Sybil and have had a vision."

"Can tell what will happen in the future, are you a future-teller?" asked Forenk.

"Well, really more of a past-teller," said Hezfytis.

"A past-teller?"

"That is correct, I tell the past."

"Can not anyone tell the past. It has already happened," said Forenk.

"No, not really, you do have to know what has happened," said Hezfytis.

"So you can tell the past without being told about it or seeing it happen yourself?"

"Yes, although sometimes it takes years to get it right." Donoxa interrupted, saying to Forenk, "We must allow Hezfytis to tell us his prophecy."

"Well, it is more like advice really. Prophecy is such a big word. I do not want to disappoint," said Hezfytis. "But let us see, we have Forenk, his mother is Thegotta, his father Mipinus, the problem with Jykee, the sword and the squirrel, stop me if I wander."

"You are good so far," said Donoxa.

"Forenk has a long road ahead and must face many challenges and suffer many loses. The first obstacle is the squirrel, the Ancestor Squirrel, a manifestation of one of the first squirrels. But you probably knew that?"

"Gerojef said something to that effect," said Donoxa, "Is seems this Squirrel Ancestor seeks revenge on Forenk."

"The humiliation of Jykee was a crushing defeat for squirrel-kind. But this squirrel is under oath to aid any agent of Mipinus, and certainly the son of the god would qualify. I would venture some other force at work perverting the squirrel's oath to ending Forenk's..., err, career."

Donoxa noticed that Forenk was growing increasingly apprehensive as Hezfytis spoke, so she interrupted and said, "Is this squirrel a lone enemy and if so what about the demons?"

"I am not sure about the demons, but I have suspicions," said Hezfytis. "The demons will not pose much of a problem once the sword is re-enchanted."

"Re-enchanted?" said Donoxa turning to Heela.

Heela nodded and said, "Yes, I thought that some power was sleeping within the sword."

Ahh, perhaps a counter-spell to hold back the power of the sword and a web of spells to hide the counter-spell from being detected," said Donoxa. "They must be powerful spells."

"Did the squirrel summons the demons?" said Forenk. Hezfytis shifted his eyes towards Forenk and said, "No, I do not think the squirrel would summons hell spawn, it would more likely attack you itself, as it did. But, Jykee had a mistress wife, a wood witch nymph by the name of Drogana and she appeared in my vision. I think Drogana may be the one seeking revenge on the son of Mipinus and a formidable enemy she is."

"A witch is summonsing demons to kill me?" said Forenk. He sat up and looked from side to side in mounting panic as if he expected an attack at any moment.

"Forenk! Be calm," said Donoxa. She waved her hands in his direction and sang, nearly whispered a spell song, "Be calm and seek, some peace in sleep."

Forenk head was filled with the lovely peaceful voice of Donoxa and it occurred to him, as he relaxed and consciousness slipped away, that it was surely a lucky break that Donoxa and Heela were sent as guardian angels to protect him considering the very seriously dangerous enemies he had so recently acquired.

35 Way Over Your Head

After waking to torchlight in a recessed sleeping chamber deep in the cave Forenk and the others were brought to the stone table they had employed the day before to eat breakfast. After the meal they were shown in to the chamber of the noxious pool of sibylline water and to meet with Hezfytis.

"Good morning all. Ah, Forenk, feeling better, are we? Slept well?" said Hezfytis from his perch on the finely carved pedestal.

Forenk found talking to a disembodied head was only slightly less stranger than yesterday. "Yes, surprisingly well under the circumstances," he said. He looked sheepishly at Donoxa as if he knew that he had been put to sleep magically, and then turned back to Hezfytis. "And yourself, Sir, did you sleep well?"

"Actually, not well, I had a headache," said Hezfytis. He waited for the attendants laughter to subside and then said, "I just could not get comfortable. I remember when I had arms and I used to think my arms were in the way of getting comfortable while lying down. They were a nuisance, I just never knew where to put the damn things, ha, ha. But of course now I would give an ear to have an arm."

"Hezfytis, is there anything you could tell us that would be helpful in aiding Forenk? What will this Drogana, the witch wife of Jykee do next? What shall we expect, what can we do?" said Heela.

Hezfytis said, "The first thing you need to do is head…," he waited for the sniggering of the attendants to cease and then said, "north. You must go north to the tower of Mouron the Enchanter."

Gerojef hooted along with the attendant monks.

Forenk asked Gerojef why he was laughing. Gerojef used his robe sleeve to dry a tear of laughter rolling down his cheek. He said, "I have heard of Mouron the Enchanter and he is also called the Stupid Wizard."

Heela said, "I am displeased with the frivolous manner in which these councils are being directed. Forenk is on a mission of great import and has treacherous foes to contend with. Gerojef, I remember your taking your duties at the sacred grove quite gravely. Do you feel that our quest is less important?"

Gerojef said, "Of course not! Was I not there when that devil attacked us? It was pointed out I have been of great assistance in Forenk's expedition." His tone changed from defensive to reflective as he peered at nothing in particular. "It is true, the demon's attack has shaken something loose in me. A weight has been lifted. The responsibilities of the Sacred Grove were solemn and required conscientious concentration and solemnity. I am free for the first time in my life!"

Hezfytis said, " You must use your head," he waited while the monks guffawed, chortled and snorted, then finished his sentence, "What combats fear better than humor?"

There was a moment of rare silence and then Hezfytis said. "However, it may prove prudent to dispense with the merriment briefly."

Hezfytis, literally the head oracle, somehow cleared his throat, pouted while his face shriveled into a dour expression and said, "I agree with Donoxa, it is likely that Drogana has placed a binding or dampening spell on the Squirrel Sword. But this I know, like the ancestor squirrel, Drogana was included in the oath to aid Mipinus. But, she is hungry for power and I have heard tales that when she lost her prestige and position those many years ago she flew into a rage and swore vengeance. In fact, in the one place in the world where she still is revered, the Ruins, the remains of a great empire from an eon ago, the tribesmen worship her as the Goddess of Vengeance. She has built up her power and has become a powerful witch of godly power."

They all watched as Hezfytis arched his brows and his eyes jumped from one to another of them, he said, "To counter her magic, you must enlist the aid of Mouron the enchanter, for only he will be able to release the powers of the sword. Mouron lives many leagues to the North in his wizard's tower. Gerojef, do you know the location of Mouron's tower?"

Gerojef rummaged around in his memory and said, "I have heard tell it lies near the Ruined Ruins. The long deserted city of a people long gone, now populated by a savage tribe from the far north, as you have said. But I have not traveled that far north."

"Yes, Mouron's tower is east of the ruins. I will see to it that you are provided with a map or better still, Thungi, my warrior monk, will guide you there," said Hezfytis.

Thungi who stood by the arched entrance to the chamber took a step forward, bent at the waist in a deep bow and said, "Yes, master, shall I prepare provisions for the journey?"

Hezfytis signaled yes by wagging his brow and Thungi, accustomed to Hezfytis facial language, dashed out sniggering to himself as he said, "Yes, master, I will get a head start."

Hezfytis ignored Thungi's impertinence, turned back to Forenk and his party of adventurers and said, "If you leave now, you could make it to the town of Squirrel Turd by sundown tomorrow."

"Squirrel Turd?" asked Forenk.

"Yes, you are deep in squirrel territory now, even this mountain was originally called Squirrel Mountain before its current name," said Hezfytis. He gazed at Forenk for a while and then said, "I will inhale the vapors again and dream once more in the oracles trance because there is something hidden from me, something sinister and cloaked from prophecy."

The severed head that was Hezfytis smiled wistfully and said, "But then life is full of astonishments. Think of a large plump ripe orange and imagine peeling the rind in one piece that winds around the outside surface of the orange. Now imagine the orange as a mystery you are trying to solve and that to solve that mystery you need to walk on that winding length of rind as it is unpeeled. You will discover the meaning of your journey is the journey itself, although many things will be reckoned with and many will be effected. Your path is the hero's path and great will be the deeds of the hero you will be!"

Hezfytis smiled and looked at Forenk expectantly. Forenk had lapsed back into his typically blank expression which hinted at confusion and left Hezfytis disappointed. He said, "Okay, allow me to pose it another way. You and your companions are tied together in fellowship, you will quest, walk this winding rind together. Perhaps you could use a questing name for your enterprise."

Gerojef pulled at his beard contemplatively while Forenk gaped dully. Heela contained her impatience but said, "I am not sure where you re going with this line of thought, Master Oracle."

Hezfytis looked at her and said, "Well, that would make you and your companions The Fellowship of the…."

Donoxa said, "Please! Do not say it!"

"Rind?"

"I do not understand," said Forenk.

Hezfytis said, "Very well then, Donoxa, I will do as you say. But how about hugging me to your bosoms then? I may be over a thousand years old and even though I do not have a body, I m still a man with needs."

Hezfytis eyes enlarged as he ogled Donoxa. "God you re incredible!" he said. "Bend over and give baby his milk, yes, baby wants his teat to feed on. Come on, would it be so bad to humor an old body-less man? I helped you out, did I not?"

Donoxa looked at Heela who shrugged her shoulders, so Donoxa picked up the head and squeezed it between her breasts.

"Oh lordy, mmm, ish goo, mmm," said Hezfytis, buried in the luxurious depths of Donoxa's bosoms. After a few minutes she put the contentedly cooing head back on the pedestal.

"My turn," said Gerojef. "Maybe some other time, we need to get a move on," Donoxa said. "Yes, you must be on your way, there are many forces at work, you will need to act swiftly before things come to a…head," said Hezfytis, saliva drooling from his lips but beaming as the chamber filled with laughter.

36 A little Famine Goes a Long Way

Thungi was waiting with provisions at dawn and the party of five left Swine Mountain and set out into the cool morning air for the march towards the enchanter's tower. Refreshed and armed with some inkling of the challenges that lay ahead, Forenk felt a sense of purpose. He discovered that he had become accustomed to marching all day and took some joy in it. At midday he joined in when Donoxa and Heela sang one of their strange songs. Even Gerojef hummed along, it was evident that he could enjoy the company if not all the details of the quest.

That night they took turns at watch while the others slept. The night passed without incident and the morning sun rose spreading warmth over the travelers as they packed up the scant camp gear and prepared to continue their march.

A sweet breeze carrying a fragrance new to Forenk, greeted them at the start of the day's hike, and he expected to find the day filled with greenery, flowers and birdsong. But soon after they had marched a little ways, the countryside began to resemble the lifeless land they had traversed on their way to Swine Mountain.

The area around Swine Mountain had had a semblance of normalcy, surrounded by a few healthy-looking trees and green grasses, but it was an island in a wasteland, for soon after leaving the area they found themselves once again amidst the gray sand and sickly trees they had passed on their way to the Oracle's caverns.

~"~

The sun was disappearing over the horizon after a full day's march when they sighted the squalid village of Squirrel Turd, an almost deserted colony of haphazardly constructed dwellings. The unpleasant village consisted of a collection of formless dung hovels and the sickly humanoid forms that haunted them.

There was something unfamiliar and hard to describe about the villagers, but repugnant and odorous came close to the mark. The few pallid residents of the ailing community noticed the newcomers and listlessly drew near like zombies. They surrounded Forenk, Heela, Donoxa, Gerojef and Thungi, who stood their ground passively.

None of the villagers were armed or looked very dangerous but one could sense the hazard in being around them. One villager, noticeably smellier than the rest of the reeking assembly, spoke in the common tongue.

"Do you have any food?"

Forenk and his companions were invited to the hetman's hut but after a brief glimpse through the door flap and a whiff of the contents, they made it apparent that they preferred to stay outdoors. A campfire was started in the center of the hamlet. After having a good look at the verminous huts and the diseased-looking rags the villagers wore Gerojef muttered something about the benefits of burning down the entire village for sanitary reasons but was ignored.

Once everyone had gathered round the fire, Donoxa ordered Thungi to surrender most of the group's provisions to the ravenous population of Squirrel Turd. The food was devoured quickly and the people of the village thanked the adventurers and chatted amiably with the quest mates. The village chief told them that the village had just survived a famine. He explained that by making sacrifices to the gods the famine had finally ended.

"What kind of sacrifices?" asked Forenk.

"We sacrificed the old, the infirm and every other man and woman, about two-thirds of the village, and now there is no longer a famine."

"Your crops and hunting game were blessed by the gods and become more bountiful?" asked Forenk.

"No," said the hetman of Squirrel Turd, "fewer mouths to feed."

37 Thungi Departs Undramatically

The party reached a good distance from Squirrel Turd before the sun had completed rising the next day. As they marched along Forenk glanced back at the diminishing huts, made even more dismal in the gray light, and said, "We never asked how the village got the name of Squirrel Turd."

"Perhaps when the village was first assembled the huts were made from squirrel dung instead of human poop," offered Gerojef.

Forenk considered Gerojef's explanation, stared expressionlessly at him for a moment and then said, "I did not see any squirrels, did anyone else?"

Heela said, "No. I think it is because we have been vigilant. But I will not let us be lulled into a false sense of security. I think we should keep a double guard, two awake at all times tonight. We will be less likely to be surprised and two lookouts can keep an eye on each other and make sure no one falls asleep on duty." She darted a glance at Gerojef, who smiled sheepishly.

Although Forenk remained on edge the entire time, the day of trekking towards their new destination passed uneventfully. There was little talk during the day and soon after dusk all except the first night watch, Heela and Gerojef were rolled up in blankets.

Forenk had a dream and in that dream, waves of thousands of squirrels migrated to some unknown destination. Forenk floated above the herds of stampeding squirrels unseen. From horizon to horizon all he could see was the squirming gray tide, a texture of squirrels as they hopped and scampered, backs rising, dipping and leaping forward and up.

Forenk fell from the sky very slowly, he watched in anguish as the uncounted squirrels stopped running and converged below him, forming a pyramid of fur and biting teeth. Just as Forenk hit the squirrel mound expecting the squirrel fangs to begin their gruesome work, he awoke ready to cry for help but he found he was still wrapped in his blanket and the morning sun peeked over a large nearby hill.

Forenk recovered from his nightmare over breakfast and after the meal of grain gruel Thungi prepared, he and Heela practiced with the sword. They had been honing Forenk's skill at every opportunity since the instruction begun.

Thungi was able to give Forenk a few pointers at handling weapons as well. He commented on how apt a pupil Forenk was, but Forenk knew that Heela was at least partially responsible for his swift advancement.

In addition to the sword practice, Donoxa had been explaining the basic principles of magic to Forenk. Much to his own surprise he had caught on fast. In just a few days he had learned to turn wet stream stones into little gray jumping frogs and campfire sparks into fireflies. The little sorcerous transformations were minor tricks but a solid beginning for a fledgling magic user. Some change was coming over Forenk and he liked it most of the time.

Thungi told the quest mates that their destination, the enchanter's tower, lay one day's march due north, at the western foot of a small isolated mountain. He said, "If you will no longer require my services, I shall return to my duties at Swine Mountain."

They thanked Thungi for his help but before he left he drew a crude map of the area. He gave the map to Gerojef and wished Forenk and his companions well, then departed, heading back the way they had come.

The remaining party trekked north. Later in the day the desolate ground gave way to more pleasant surroundings. Fields of green scrub grass replaced the brownish clumps of spindly weeds. Copses of healthy trees could be seen in the distance. It was going on to be a beautiful day.

As the environment became more idyllic Forenk's cheered up and began to relax. He thought to himself how promising it was to becoming a swordsman, a magician, a hero! If he had not lived every moment leading up to this one he would not have believed it possible, limited as his travels had been before he left Pig Whistle a few weeks ago.

In his imagination he conjured up images of the party roving the world over, traveling through strange lands, meeting strange peoples and defeating very strange enemies. After all, except for a few sleepless nights, being terrified most of the time and having one of his testicles bitten off, it had been a great adventure. Of course there was Bahjob's death and they had not come up against the witch goddess Drogana directly, yet.

38 Drogana The Witch Goddess

As they went over the crest of the next hill they saw a woman standing in the shadow of a gnarly tree. By her side sat a very large animal and its body from a distance resembling a cross between a lion and a mastiff except for the beast's head which looked near human. As he drew closer, shivers rippled through Forenk when he saw the animal wore a weird grin on the too human macabre features.

The woman smirked, malicious dark eyes shining out of her perfectly beautiful face. She wore all black and her long raven tresses were crowned with a garland of yellow and black herbs.

"This is not good, she is emanating power," said Gerojef. "Stand your ground," said Heela as she smoothly unsheathed the Squirrel Sword.

"This will be Drogana, the witch," said Donoxa, "here to see Forenk and his company for herself."

"How do you know that? Is that beast a natural one?" said Forenk, attempting to whisper with a waver in his voice.

"Because of everything we have learned to this point," said Donoxa.

Gerojef said, "No, that thing next to the witch is not of this world's natural beasts, a demon, maybe her familiar." Gerojef keep his voice low so as to not be overheard by the woman in black.

They came to a stop ten paces from the witch.

Drogana looked at Heela, sizing her up and said, "Pulling a sword on an unarmed woman all alone in the wilds? Dear me, what barbaric times we have fallen on." Her voice was sweet and frail sounding. She gestured daintily with her hands, feigning distress, but her eyes were piercing and sardonic.

"You are not alone. Some hell-borne beast stands by your side, your familiar or a new paramour?" said Heela.

Drogana ignored the slight to reply cooly saying,

Drogana and Her Pet

"Oh, do not tell me my little lap pet here frightens the brave adventurers." Her features grew darker and the sound of thunder came from clouds that seemed to suddenly roil overhead.

The animal by they were discussing smiled, opening its mouth to reveal rows of yellow pointy fangs. Its eyes burned with a wicked intelligence as it rose from it's sitting position. It was the size of a pony, only leaner and muscular.

"What do you want, Drogana, or should I ask, how do you propose to get it?" said Donoxa.

The witch looked through them like her eyes saw a different world and she spoke to herself mostly when she said, "You have heard of me, interesting, but not surprising. Yes, I want the sword, it is my husband's! And, what I want is for you to all to go back where you came from and leave the sword with me." The thunder grew louder and far off a bolt of lightning flashed in the darkened sky.

"Have you forgotten the covenant, Jykee swore an oath…, said Gerojef, before getting cut off by Drogana.

Hissing, Drogana said, "Shut up you old traitorous fool! Have you forgotten which god you serve? What care I for promises made in time out of mind. Give me the sword!" For a moment her features contorted in rage but she regained control of her emotions and her eyes lost their vacant stare.

Drogana focused on Forenk and said, "You," her voice turned to silk, "are a very handsome, young man. I have heard such delicious rumors of your romantic prowess." She beckoned him and her robe parted as if by accident to reveal the beauty within, a beauty that made Forenk's cheeks burn.

Forenk could see her point, she was a god's wife, and a very beautiful one, he would be glad to give her the Squirrel Sword, especially if she insisted on the carnal pleasures the other divinities had.

"Forenk," said Donoxa, "Drogana is casting a spell on you." Donoxa pointed at the witch goddess and murmured a song, an incantation, that interrupted the glamour spell that the witch goddess had cast on Forenk.

Forenk felt as if he had woken from a dream and for a moment Forenk he could see Drogana's true aspect. A putrescent foulness in the general shape and features of a woman stood where the beautiful woman in black had stood. Flies and lesser carrion swirled around it's rotting flesh. Then the image was gone and the beautiful woman in black was back.

Drogana peered at Donoxa and said, "You are not a true mortal, you are some divine menial and you have skill with the sorcerous arts, but," the volume and tone of Drogana voice grew to a shrill as she screamed at Donoxa, "HAVE YOU POWER!" The witch pointed her fingers at Donoxa and an a bolt of lightning shot down from the electric storm overhead and hurled Donoxa backwards, a cry barely escaping her lips.

Drogana, eyes grotesquely enlarged with madness, turned to the weird beast beside her and laughing wildly said, "Fetch the sword, my pet! Fetch the sword for your mistress, but kill them all first!"

The monster cat-dog stepped forward, somehow increasing in size as it approached. Heela stepped in front of Forenk holding the Squirrel Sword before her. Gerojef, although clearly frightened, began to chant, calling on the spirits of the woods.

Forenk chanced a look behind to see Donoxa on her back, smoke curling from her unmoving body. He turned back at the witch's frenzied laughter in time to witness Heela swing the sword at the creature.

With uncanny dexterity the beast managed to dodge Heela's sword swing and then snap unnaturally wide jaws at her. Heela matched the demon beast's extraordinary speed and agility. She swung the blade in a blinding zigzag that ripped open the breast of the demon. It howled in anger and pain, the wide gash in its chest spurted smoke and green ichor, the demon's blood.

"Bitch, I will chew your heart out for that," said the demon. Its voice a weird deep speaking roar. It snapped angrily but not warily enough and Heela lobbed off a piece of skull and an ear. The monstrosity cried out again, it lurched pitifully, losing control of its body, it said to Drogana, "Mistress, the sword-wielding bitch has slain me."

Heela struck again while the demon spoke to Drogana and the beast's head thumped to the ground followed by it's grossly inflated body. Without hesitation Heela ran towards the witch goddess to finish the battle.

Drogana appeared stunned for a moment by the loss of her demon familiar but pointed her fingers and a bolt of lightening struck out at Heela just before she reached her. Heela's body flew back towards Forenk who was desperately waiting for a chance to take action. He resisted the urge to look at Heela's burnt black body and without taking his eyes off the witch, lifted the sword from where it had fallen.

At that moment Gerojef's summons was complete and the roots of the tree that Drogana stood beneath shot out tendrils that wound themselves around the witch's legs and upwards around her torso and arms. She laughed maniacally and spoke in an arcane tongue as Forenk inched towards her on quaking legs.

The tree roots wrapped and tightened around Drogana until she was completely bound, her arms helpless. In a demented screeching voice she cast a spell. Fire sprang up out of nowhere and spread around her, wilting the leaves of the tree and forcing Forenk to recoil before the heat of the blaze. Drogana, engulfed in flames was unharmed, impervious to the magic flames. She continued her uncontrolled laugher as the tree's tendril-like roots withdrew smoking. The fire subsided as soon as Drogana was free.

The witch goddess stared into Forenk's eyes and he watched as the crazed reptilian gaze was replaced by sultry invitation. In a husky feminine voice smooth as fine velvet, Drogana said, "Give me the Squirrel Sword and then you may go on your way with your friends." She smiled sweetly and her robe parted again. Forenk recalled the decaying being he had seen when Donoxa had broken the charm spell. But Forenk felt compelled to disregard what he had seen with his own eyes and obey her as he closed the few remaining yards between them.

"Good boy. Give it to me," said Drogana sweetly, her face wholesome and innocent. She opened her arms as to embrace Forenk.

Forenk said, "Here, TAKE IT!" and thrusted the blade between her perfectly formed breasts. Red smoking blood spurted out and Drogana stared down at it in disbelief. Forenk shoved the blade in deeper and felt it bite into the tree behind the witch.

Drogana's head rose twitching. She smiled and said, "Very clever, you fooled old Drogana, did you boy?" The sound of her voice had changed into an ancient harpy's that grated on Forenk's nerves and he guessed that this was the real voice of Drogana.

"Ha, hee, ha, hee. You have done well for yourself, have you not? That little curse I put on you did not finish you off. Your parents take good care of their only son." She smiled at Forenk's reaction to the news.

The mystery of the curse plaguing him all but the last three weeks of his life was solved. The sight of the mortally wounded witch casually speaking shocked and sickened Forenk, but he still savored the taste of a well-deserved revenge.

Drogana said, "It seems that you win for now, but I will have the sword back and then I will see you in hell! Ha, hee, ha, hee!" She convulsed violently, puking smoldering blood and her corrupt form slouched over dead on the sword that pinned it to the tree.

Forenk turned, fell to his knees and vomited.

~"~

When Forenk recovered, he looked around, avoiding the ghastly sight of Drogana impaled by the Squirrel Sword. Gerojef slumped in an exhausted heap where he had stood his ground earlier and cast the spell that had allowed Forenk to approach the witch. Forenk walked towards Gerojef fearing the worst. Wisps of smoke still rose from Heela's body and Forenk nearly gagged from the stench of burning flesh that reached his nose. A little further behind the body of Heela lay Donoxa. Both bodies were charred and unrecognizable. Forenk felt himself go numb to hold off the wave of grief.

He was startled and relieved to hear Gerojef's croaking voice say, "I am sorry Forenk, sorry for our friends. I shall return to the grove, I can do no more."

Forenk turned to him but their eyes did not meet. Although Gerojef had acted with bravery in the face of a formidable foe, like Forenk, he had soiled himself during the battle and now he sat staring ahead, an old man, ready to die.

"Will you not go to the enchanter's tower?" said Forenk. He held back a sob. Gerojef did not answer and Forenk, suddenly all alone, let the tears flow.

After a while Forenk got up and walked back to retrieve the sword. He let the putrid corpse slide to the ground. The tree was singed from the fire and a sickly gray where the body of the witch goddess had touched it.

Using the sword and his hands as a shovel, Forenk managed to dig shallow graves for his lost companions far from the tree where the witches body lay. When he returned for the bodies, Forenk took the squirrel tail from Heela's belt, somehow the tail of the Ancestor Squirrel was merely singed.

He silently composed a short prayer while he filled the graves and when finished, he sank to his knees exhausted, in every way possible, to grieve. He swore he would carry out whatever mission Heela and Donoxa were sent to help him with, whatever that ended up being.

39 A Dreamy Reunion

It was growing dark when Forenk selected a campsite and collected some scraggly brush and sad looking firewood to start a fire. After herding Gerojef to a comfortable spot near the campfire, the old druid had become quiet and passive, Forenk covered him with a blanket. Forenk then unrolled his threadbare blanket and lay down, fatigued beyond imagining, yet with sword in hand ready to fend off all transgressors, and immediately fell into the deep sleep.

Forenk dreamt. He wandered aimlessly through endless landscapes. Horrendous creatures and scheming gods glimpsed in the trees and clouds avoided his gaze. On he walked without purpose or destination until he thought he heard voices in the distance, then familiar laughter a little bit closer.

He turned to see Heela and Donoxa appear before him, alive and delicately beautiful as ever.

"I thought the Drogana killed you," said Forenk, numbly. They laughed and like an echo on the edge of memory their voices harmonized and they said, "Mortal death cannot come to eternal spirits, Forenk. Drogana has only destroyed the bodies we wore. Your father Mipinus may create new ones for us. We shall see you again in the waking world."

They hugged and kissed Forenk as a great sense of relief swept over him. Embarrassed at not being able to keep tears from his eyes he said, "I thought I lost you, that you were no more."

"No, sweet friend, we may be able to return to you at the end of your journey to fulfill the prophecy if it is the will of the gods. Although your fate is your own now, our strengths are your strengths and we will always be with you in spirit at the very least."

They began to laugh again and although Forenk was not quite sure what they meant, he felt consoled. He trusted what they said without knowing what they intended. In the short period that he had shared their company their riddle-laden chatter had eventually resolved itself into the understandable more than once.

"What do I do now?" said Forenk, guessing what the answer would be. Because it was a dream or because they knew that he knew the answer, they did not reply and the two lovely smiling faces faded into the dreamy landscape.

Forenk rose with the sun, sat up, drank heartily from his water bag and wondered if Heela and Donoxa had really contacted him in his dream. Unheard of things, the stuff of legend and the supernatural, were becoming ordinary to him, so it was likely more real than dream.

Gerojef still slept, so Forenk prepared a modest breakfast meal before waking him gently.

The druid looked rested but remained quiet while they ate. Afterwards he studied Forenk thoughtfully and said, "Are you ready to travel on?"

"So you will continue with me after all?" said Forenk brightly.

"I suppose finishing the northward leg of our journey would not be out of the question." He managed a grin but Forenk could see in Gerojef's ancient eyes that the events of the day before had almost broken him.

40 Mouron Than Off

The sun was setting once more after a long day's march when in the distance Forenk managed to spy the faded green peaked roof of a tower just topping the high branches amongst the trees ahead of them. The woods had thickened as they headed north and formed a forest when they arrived at the base of a great hill. The mortared stone tower sat on a gentle slope surrounded by trees. Gerojef had been expounding on the insights of his life's experiences when Forenk noted the structure.

Gerojef said, "The tower of Mouron the Enchanter. Less than half a league I would guess. I have never traveled this far north and now realize how long I had been tending the sacred grove. To think all those years have led up to you coming along and the very strange quest we have undertaken. Mind you, I had dealt with the odd monster and spirit. No one could reach my age and avoid them in this world. But to battle the demons of hell and emerge victorious. That is singular!"

Gerojef looked sadly at Forenk for a moment, then said, "For the most part before your arrival I was becoming irritable and tiresome of the responsibility of running the Sacred Grove with the sorry lot of supplicants supposedly there to aid me. Then of course all the idiotic antics and whining."

Were they that bad?" said Forenk.

Well, that last part was actually about you," said Gerojef, adding quickly, "but you have changed dramatically!

Gerojef smiled wistfully, "Everything changes so quickly as you age. I remember being a bit bored when I was a youngster or at any rate, something like bored. The feeling of there being lots of time and that life goes on endlessly passes swiftly and then you catch glimpses of the end and you learn to appreciate every day that you have. I think I will not let things upset me for any longer than they insist upon upsetting me. I will not spend my last days in consternation."

Gerojef turned to Forenk and waited a moment for a reply then asked him, "What do you think, my young man?"

Forenk, who, except when his life was being threatened, did feel there was lots of time and believed life went on endlessly, only identified with half of what Gerojef was saying, but he nodded his head and said, "I suppose that is better than being miserable."

They had come to a clearing in the foliage and Forenk said, "The tower is taller than I imagined, taller than the trees."

Forenk took in the area surrounding the tower and the absence of activity was the first thing he noticed. There was a covered well, a few tools in a one-walled shed and an untended garden with unordered rows and plots of herbs and vegetables. No longer in use, the remains of a two-wheeled wagon covered with rotting shreds of canvas lay off to one side.

The tower itself gave the impression of being ancient and belonging to another age. Forenk felt the weight of history residing in it's crumbling masonry. Moss-covered stone showed through disintegrating mortar in many places. The tower's base was eight yards wide and shot straight up for twenty yards to a sloping ceramic tiled rooftop, much of it in disrepair. The unadorned stone of the tower was broken only by rectangular windows. A stout wooden door with iron bands barred unwelcome entry and Forenk noticed that there was a key in the door lock, a device he had never seen until he visited the city of Eysor.

"Firmly constructed," said Gerojef, "I would venture this structure has weathered many a stormy season."

"Gerojef, there is a key in the door, do you think there is any one here? It could be abandoned. The garden has not been looked after. Shall we go in? It is getting dark and the wind is picking up," Said Forenk.

Gerojef backed away from the tower looking up and said, "Let us call first and see if anyone hears us. I do not fancy bursting in on a wizard uninvited."

Gerojef yelled out the common wayfarer's greetings and after a minute a head poked out of the uppermost casement. The head was adorned with a long pointy hat that almost blew off in the mounting evening wind. The owner of the head grabbed his hat just in time to prevent it from sailing away on the swirling air currents.

The wizard peered down at them and said something but they could not make out his words because of the distance and the growing rush of the wind. He motioned to them to stay put, ducked back in and two minutes later popped his pointy-hatted head out of a window only a few yards above them.

The enchanter stared at them with a mixture of bewilderment and delight, "Oh, haloo down there, good day, oh my, its almost night, is not it. I am sorry, but I do not recollect, that is, have we met before? My memory is not what is once was, well actually, I do not remember what it once was. Hmm, I would invite you inside but I seem to have locked myself in. Its fortunate that you came along, you may be able to help me. A ladder perhaps might be in order or some sort of rope, lets see. I could build a pulley, oh no, my wood tools are down in the shed, maybe you would be kind enough to build a pulley and then we could hoist you up here and in for tea."

"The key is in the lock," said Forenk, pointing to the door, "Could we not just open it?"

"What? Well, is that where it is? It is not doing me any good down there is it? I can not open the door from outside. Oh, how ridiculous, you could open the door. I am a bit scatterbrained these days, or perhaps I have always been, honestly, I do not recollect." The enchanter stopped as if he had had enough of his own rambling dialog and added very soberly, "I will be right down."

"I suppose you will need to unlock the door," the wizard said moments later from behind the locked wooden door. Forenk turned the key gingerly as if expecting it to break but it clicked instead and the door swung open.

Mouron the Enchanter was of average height or less and slightly round of shape. He wore a well-made but aging robe of powder blue decorated with fading symbols and a matching short brimmed pointed hat. His manner was courteous and

Mouron the Enchanter

mildly excited.

"Ah, that is a relief, I have been stuck in here for over a week or was it two weeks? I thought I had discovered the secret of immortality but needed an herb from my garden when I discovered I had locked myself in. I probably should teach myself the open portal spell first, ha, ha, can you imagine being immortal and stuck in the tower, yes." The wizard laughed and noticing he did so alone, stopped and suddenly said, "The name is Mouron, by the way, and whom do I have the honor of thanking for my rescue?"

"I am Forenk, I was until a few weeks ago, a pig farmer," said Forenk. ,and this is Gerojef, druid and former Master of the of the Sacred Oak Grove.

Mouron looked impressed by Gerojef's title and said to him, "And what business brings the Master of the of the Sacred Oak Grove and Forenk, Pig Farmer to the abode of Mouron the Enchanter?"

Before Gerojef could launch into a speech, Forenk drew out the Squirrel Sword and it seemed to shine even in the growing darkness. He held the sword up like a torch and said, "I am also the Son of Mipinus and Thegotta and this is the Sacred Squirrel Sword, the sword of Jykee, the woodland deity and the God of Squirrels."

Forenk briefly recounted the situation as he understood it thus far and Gerojef added a detail and an opinion or two without becoming tedious. Forenk concluded by saying, "Hezfytis, the head…, the Oracle of Swine Mountain advised us to come to you because he and," Forenk hesitated for a moment, then continued, "and former companions of mine, believed the witch Drogana wove a spell on the sword to keep its powers restrained. Hezfytis believed you could restore the sword to its past quality by re-enchanting it."

Forenk recognized that he was speaking on his own behalf where one of the others would have done so before.

The wizard had taken it all in without a question or word of reply. When he was sure Forenk was finished he stood back and waved them into the tower. "Well, do come in and we will start a fire, light some candles and see what an old wizard can conjure up as a meal for his well-met guests."

As they were led inside, Gerojef said, "I am curious, how did you manage to lock the door from the outside?"

Mouron made a half embarrassed smile and said, "I am afraid I do not remember."

41 The Salad Dressing of Sleep

After seating his guest in a dark wooden booth between an array of dark wooden shelves lining the inner stone wall of the structure the enchanter began to prepare the meal he had offered to Forenk and Gerojef.

The dust-covered shelves and cupboards wound around every section of the inside wall of the tower except for where the door, fireplace and table booth stood. Sniffing the air Forenk noted that the odors were only mildly alarming.

He saw, arrayed in no discernible order, bottles in a variety of textures, shapes and colors. Containers made of all assortment of glass of every hue and metals like bronze, lead and iron. There were small clay and woven baskets and twine bundled sheafs filled with herbs, leaves and grasses. One tall shelf was crammed with pig skin scrolls.

The insides of the bottles revealed small mammals, reptiles and amphibian. Some held animal body parts like bat ears and wings others held insects Forenk had never beheld. He stared at a bottle filled with small eyes of some unfortunate creature because the little eyes stared back. He turned around to alert the others and decided that Mouron was most likely aware of the moving eyes in the bottle.

Mouron had turned to tending ancient looking utensils around the stone fireplace to heat up some gruel. A short time later Forenk discovered that the gruel was tasty if unidentifiable and went very well with the tea sweetened with honey and a kind of flat hard cake that Mouron served afterwards.

They ate and afterwards settled back into the booths heavy wooden benches to discuss the business of the sword. Forenk, at the wizard's request, repeated the story of his adventures and travails from the beginning. He told of his life in Pig Whistle, meeting the two female companions and their adventures together. He told of his first sea voyage with Black Thumb and his crew, leaving out certain details, and of meeting the sea goddess, Mormoomi. He recalled her riddle-portent and repeated it for Mouron.

Look to the goddess of pigs for a sign
Sword of the squirrel
bring home to the swine

Forenk went on to say, "We found a sign at the temple in Eysor, near the statue of Thegotta, but I do not think that it is the one from Mormoomi's foretoken. Unless, by finding it and, erm, having some misfortunate business with a bell, being banished, directed north and running into Gerojef and the sword, I suppose that could have been the sign."

Forenk paused and look back across the tower to the little moving eyes in the bottle, they were still watching him. He said, "I am fairly certain that I need to bring the sword back to Pigland, my home, or at least that is what I intend to do unless it means something else."

Forenk looked hopefully at Mouron, but the wizard had fallen asleep. He turned to Gerojef whose sudden snoring woke Mouron.

"Oh, so your sign was, a bell, no, I m afraid I have lost the thread of the sequence of events," said the somewhat startled wizard.

Forenk, speaking loud enough to be heard over Gerojef's gurgling snore, repeated what the wizard had missed and continued his narrative of the events leading up to them arriving at Mouron's Tower. Forenk had healed in spirit since speaking with Donoxa and Heela in his dream but when he spoke of the demon and squirrel attack the dull pain in his groin grew and he squirmed in his seat. Lastly he spoke of the brutal slaying of his companions in the deadly encounter with Drogana. Mouron waited till Forenk was finished retelling his tale and then got up and bustled around the tower from shelf to shelf collecting enigmatic ingredients and piling them on the long wooden table that occupied the center of the tower. He then proceeded to stir the liquids together and grind the dry components in a mortar with a pestle. His efforts produced a vial of liquid that he poured over the powdered concoction which immediately began to smoke profusely.

Forenk watched Mouron with curiosity and finally said, “Are you preparing some alchemical potion to counter Drogana’s dampening spell on the sword?”

“What’s that? Oh no, it is just a salad dressing,” the wizard said without looking up, then apologetically added, “Wait, oh yes, it is a potion for the purpose of restoring the sword. I was thinking of making salad dressing, something in the smell of one of the ingredients reminded me of a favorite dish, but this potion, that I prepare now, is for the sword.”

“You seem to know the alchemical arts well, Enchanter,” said Gerojef.

“Many enchantments require the use of material elements as well as knowledge of the true speech,” said Mouron. He covered the foul smelling solution and put it on one of the crowded shelves lining the walls.

Forenk said, “Donoxa told me that true speech is the language of the gods.”

Gerojef nodded in agreement.

Mouron turned to Forenk and said, “The story of your adventures are enlightening. I know of Drogana, the witch wife of Jykee, the Woodland God. She is a great evil spirit intent on gaining control of this land. My familiar sensed her magic early yesterday.”

“Your familiar?” asked Forenk.

“Yes, Zook, my familiar, he is invisible to the eye. He is a spirit to be exact,” replied Mouron.

Forenk looked around the shadowy chamber as if he might be able to discern some telltale sign of a ghost’s presence.

Mouron said, “What was it, I ca not recall my train of thought, I am rather easily confounded as you can see. Ah, yes, Zook, my familiar sensed Drogana casting a detection spell, which I promptly dispelled. Was that after or before she found you?” Mouron put his finger to his lips for a moment, thinking. “Hmm I believe you have thwarted her schemes for the moment by destroying the antique husk she was born into." He thought for a moment longer and added, "It could have been a possessed body she corrupted."

Gerojef, woken and stirring to consciousness by the vile smell of the enchanter's brew, said, "Hmm, Drogana could re-manifest or steal a body to pursue her plan to wreak vengeance on Forenk and win back the Squirrel Sword."

"She needs no body to work her evil witchcraft," Mouron said. "There is no telling what she will do next. Her dark sorceries, as you have seen, summon demons to do her bidding. Forenk represents the enduring lineage of her hated enemy Mipinus. Perhaps she was building her influence in the world and was satisfied while Forenk here was living under her curse and the sword was safe in the Sacred grove. But with Forenk out and err…, spreading the seed of his divine father's kindred and the Squirrel Sword in his hands. Well, to simplify the matter, her goal is to end the line and regain the sword."

Gerojef said, "The Squirrel Sword is a symbol of sovereignty, it may nominally represent her right to dominion over these lands. I think she will either come to get it or send someone…, or something."

Mouron nodded and said, "She will seek retribution for her humiliation by Forenk as well as to regain the sword. You have made a powerful enema."

"Do you mean enemy?" asked Forenk.

Mouron said, "Yes, I meant enemy. What did I say?"

Forenk said, "I was warned by Drogana that she would take the sword and see me in hell."

Mouron said, "Well my boy, we will do our best to prevent that!" He continued to forage through the shelves and bumped his head on an open cupboard. As if being struck in the head jogged his memory, Mouron said, "There is a tribe that live in the ruins west of here. Zook, my familiar, has observed them worship Drogana as the Goddess of Vegetables, I meant to say Vengeance. Sorry, I am thinking of food again."

Mouron shook his head, removed his hat and rubbed the spot that had been hit by the cupboard door. He said, "Drogana is very powerful and cunning. She will most likely use every contrivance at her command to achieve her ends."

"Do these tribesmen pose a threat to us?" said Gerojef.

"I fear they would do her bidding," said Mouron. He cleared away the bowls and cups and lifted one of the burning candleholders illuminating the space, it's wavering candlelight casting dancing shadows on the dark wooden shelves and cupboards and the gray stone walls above them.

Mouron said, "Enough troubling talk for one day. Allow me to show you sleeping cots. On the morrow we will…, what was it?" For a second the wizard looked at Forenk quizzically, but before Forenk could answer, he smiled reassuringly and said, "Oh yes, restore the sword's powers."

They thanked the absent-minded enchanter then followed him up the winding stair that dominated the center of the tower to their sleeping quarters. Being inside, behind the thick walls of the tower was reassuring, and the enchanter speaking so matter-of-factly about dispelling Drogana's black magic eased Forenk's apprehensions. He slept soundly and nightmare free.

42 Some Enchanted Scheming

"How does magic work?" Mouron repeated Forenk's question. He turned as he finished, the sword bound in blades of grasses and vine, herbs, powders of many colors and odors for the ritual. He stood, stroking his long gray and white streaked beard, longer even than Gerojef's, and closed one eye then tapped his foot, as if it might help him think clearly.

After a considerable amount of time Mouron said, "That depends on a great number of variables, in this case, I wrapped the sword in the materials of the woodland, this vegetable and mineral matter, is association through contagion. It gives me power over the essences of the world, power derived from the Woodland spirits and the god, Jykee."

Mouron looked quizzical for a moment and then said, "In any case, Hezfytis believed it was better that I re-enchant the weapon. What were we speaking of, ah yes, magic, now beforehand, last night that is, before retiring, I referred to my tomes, I seem to need very little sleep these days, now that I think about it, I do not recall if I have ever needed very much sleep in the past."

A blank look once again overtook Mouron and Forenk, who guessed that the old wizard had once again lost his train of thought said, "You were saying that you referred to your tomes before retiring last night."

"Oh yes, my tomes, accumulated esoteric arcana collected over the years, I use them only as reference, really. Each enchantment is unique and I must find the correct combination of steps to reach the formula. The potion I had prepared earlier, last night, will open up portals of energy in the fabric of the world to my authority and when I pour the potion on the sword, I will be able to give direction to those forces through the ritual we now perform. Under my control the mystic powers will locate and cast out Drogana's dampening spell."

“Is there is a chance of failure?” asked Forenk, apprehension creeping into his voice, fearing the wizard would forget where he was in the ritual halfway through the spell.

Gerojef said, “Perhaps we should let Mouron perform the ritual without distraction.”

Mouron said to Gerojef, “That is quite all right, thank you, the questions actually help me stay focused, otherwise, as you may have noticed, I tend to be forgetful.”

Mouron turned back to Forenk and said, “Much like life in general, when attempting to influence the laws of the world, there is always the possibility of the unexpected. But be not distressed, young Forenk, this is familiar work. I would be amazed if there were a bewitchment I could not locate and dispel.”

Mouron’s confidence satisfied Forenk, who watched as the enchanter etched a circle of symbols into the ground there in the shade of the tool shed. Mouron described the symbols as yore-glyphs, the representation of true speech, the first tongue and the language of the gods. Forenk looked at the very strange language symbols and noted they were unlike the samples of other writing he had seen. The glyphs glowed faintly and moved when he was not looking directly at them. An aura of power emanated from the runes.

Mouron placed the greenery-wrapped sword in the center of the glyphs and stood back. The glow from the symbols seemed to converge and merge on the sword until it shone iridescently. The enchanter poured the potion he had prepared the previous night on the sword. A puff of smoke hissed noisily and sent up odorous fumes that forced Forenk to reel back. Mouron spoke first in a quick whisper and then louder until he shouted in a language that gave the listeners the impression of their ears being twisted from the inside.

There was a breaking noise like that of shattering pottery that resolved into a long flawless note of music that reminded Forenk of the Pig Whistle town ensemble, three would-be musicians who gathered to play at the festivals; they had produced such a note by accident on one occasion. Droplets of light fell like confetti over the sword. Mouron sighed heavily after his exertion and he said, “It is done, the diminishing spell of the witch is gone.”

Forenk, at the wizard’s signal, unwrapped the sword, and looked on it in marvel for it gleamed with mysterious light and when he lifted it, the blade pulsed with warm vibrations in his hands. Hefting it from hand to hand and then waving it around in mock combat. Forenk said, “It is heavier, but somehow easier to wield, it feels like part of me!”

Gerojef said, “You have no idea what a transformation you have undergone, Forenk. You positively resemble a hero, where once a.” Gerojef hesitated for a moment, smiled and said, “Well, let us just say that you appear prepared for the future.”

Forenk was well pleased by the unprecedented compliment from the Druid and he felt a new affection for the old man. The urgency and threats temporarily forgotten, the remaining hours of the day passed pleasurably listening to Mouron and Gerojef’s illuminating anecdotes. Although Mouron had to halt often to recall details.

Forenk was shown the finer points of a number of simple spells, extending his understanding of the magic Donoxa had taught him. His favorite spell was turning a breeze into a fire large enough to light a torch. Mouron told him that everyone was capable of learning magic but that few had the temperament to learn. Most will believe themselves unqualified to learn and thereby they will not. You must allow yourself to understand magic. It is a natural part of the world.

Gerojef added, “Just as when you left Pig Whistle, the world only seemed to change, it is in fact not changed, but you have gained knowledge of the world and that knowledge makes the world seem different. The world is larger, wilder, more colorful than you understood when you lived in a remote pig farming village.”

“That is true, but I do not understand how that relates to magic,” said Forenk.

“Well, do not expect to grasp every concept at first, you are doing well, but age and experience are the great teachers,” said Gerojef, winking at Mouron.

"I am afraid I do not see the connection either, the idea has merit though, does it not?" said Mouron turning to Forenk who agreed heartily.

Gerojef decided it was prudent to ask for supper at that point and they retired into the tower where Mouron served them some of last night's meal, which tasted even better than it had the night before. Forenk wondered if it might be squirrel stew, but thought it better not too ask.

"It is possum pudding," said an unfamiliar voice.

43 A Spirited Dinner Conversation

Forenk looked up from the bowl and looked at Mouron and Gerojef. Gerojef continued to eat and wore some of the gruel they were dining on in his beard.

"Something wrong Forenk?" asked Mouron noticing that Forenk had stopped eating and was looking around the room for something.

"Did you just say something about this being possum pudding?" asked Forenk.

The wizard said, "No, I did not say that, but that indeed is what the stew is."

"I thought I heard someone say it was possum pudding," said Forenk.

"Are you capable of reading minds?" asked Mouron.

I never have been, but this was…," Forenk paused to consider, "now that you mention it, the voice could have been in my head," he said.

"Yes, it is in your head, I am talking to you through your mind," said the mystery voice in his head. Forenk spilled his bowl of gruel across the surface of the heavy table, nearly over turning it as he jumped to his feet.

Gerojef started up from a ladle full of gruel and growled, "What is it?"

Mouron stared blankly for a moment then waved his hands over the table. Blue-violet sparkles fell from the ceiling above the table area. The shiny color dots outlined a small man or child's shape floating above the bench next to where Forenk had sat.

"There!" yelled Forenk pointing to the small man shape suspended in the air just above the bench.

"That is Zook, my familiar," said Mouron. "Is it he that you can hear? Are you speaking to him." Mouron turned to the color spark outlined shape and said, "Zook, are you communing with Forenk?"

Forenk heard the voice again, as Zook said to him, "Yes, please tell the mighty enchanter, it is I, Zook, his servant, bound to service. For some reason, I knew you would be able to hear me, which is strange because the wizard must go through a ceremony to communicate with me, but I am can signal him like so."

A luminescence glowed where Zook floated for a moment. Gerojef coughed a bit of the stew out and began to struggle out of his chair fearing mischief.

"Do not be alarmed," said the enchanter, "that is how my familiar contacts me, however, I do not know if the signal is merely a warning."

Forenk related what Zook had told him and Mouron performed the ceremony to verify that it was indeed his spirit familiar and not some trick of the witch Drogana or one of her evil minions.

The ceremony consisted of Mouron tracing glyphs in the air and speaking under his breath in the language that was still mostly unintelligible but beginning to become familiar to Forenk. He had learned a few words from Donoxa and Gerojef and used them to perform his minor magic feats.

The wizard sprinkled something dusty from a small pouch he had produced from the folds of his voluminous robe.

Zook said, "He must have some kind of divine hearing. I used no magic, but rather just knew that Forenk could hear me."

Gerojef smiled, recognizing spirit communication, although his speciality was communing with the living spirits of nature and the wild, not men and their kin after death had claimed them.

Zook continued speaking to Mouron, "I have set your wards as you instructed and hid them well, Master. I have not discovered the witch playing tricks on us yet."

Mouron concluded that Zook was indeed who he claimed to be and furthermore that Forenk had some unanticipated power to speak to spirits. The enchanter gave his spirit familiar the okay to continue his chat with Forenk.

Gerojef asked Forenk if he would try talking to Zook by

thinking the words and not saying them out loud. "You may be in mind speech with him."

Forenk tried talking to Zook with his mouth closed and after a few tries managed to only think and not mumble out loud.

"I can hear you," said Zook. "So, how did you like the stew?"

"Very well, although I would never had guessed it was possum. I have never tasted possum cooked and spiced like that before," said Forenk out loud. "You called it possum pudding, is a pudding considered a stew? In Pig Whistle puddings tend to be thicker."

While Zook and Forenk discussed recipes Mouron left the kitchen gallery to go up the tower stairs and returned shortly afterwards. He held what looked like a very flat pan with a handle and a shiny side, he extended the hand holding the object towards Forenk.

Forenk looked at the thing in Mouron's hand, it glimmered like the torches nearby but less bright. Forenk looked closer and saw his reflection in it. "It is like looking into a calm pool of water, What is it?"

Forenk craned his neck around the back of the mirror to see if it might expose the secret of reflection. The enchanter laughed and said, "It is a magic mirror, a little something I concocted a while back. It has a spirit sight spell bound into it. In it you can see the invisible. Hold it up so, aim it where Zook sits and you will see him."

Gerojef ah-ed at the mirror, "Lovely, to be able to see spirits."

Forenk did as the wizard instructed and a chill ran thru him. There sat a semi-translucent but otherwise pleasant looking young man not much above his own age. He had shaggy brown hair and was dressed in well-woven pants, shirt and vest. He was only half Forenk's height however and so the first thing Forenk thought to ask was, "Are spirits smaller then men? Do you shrink when you die?"

"No," replied Zook, "I am one of the Edan, a hill dwarf

or half-folk as men are wont to call us."

Forenk had heard rumors of small people creatures, collectively referred to as fairy folk by Piglanders. He noticed that Zook's ears were pointy.

Topics came and went and the conversation lasted until it grew dark and it was time for Mouron to prepare another round of the possum pudding. The stew had boiled down quite a bit and was getting thicker and starting to resemble a proper pudding.

They drank of the same spicy tea the wizard had served the previous evening. That too was getting a bit thick but tasted all the better for it. They all ate, except for Zook, but Forenk discovered he could eat and think at the same time. So they kept up the lively chat until they had told each other almost everything there was to know about the other.

"I lived in the hills beneath the Mountains of Heaven, far to the north and only a few days from the Devil's Forest, where the devil's demon daughters are queen-generals of armies that continue his battle in the Never-Ending War," said Zook.

Forenk thought about bringing up the Grand Pork Festival, remembered the incident with his pig Harbo that had set him crying into the forest and decided better against it. He told Zook about his travels since then and did not seem to have much more to say about himself, so instead he asked Zook, "Why did you leave home in the first place?"

"I would like to say I was overtaken by wanderlust for adventure and romance and left my home for destinations unknown. But I died and became a spirit and only then realized that I had not appreciated my short life very much. It was my will to experience a little more, even as a spirit, before I made the journey of no return to the gray lands of the dead. That desire to stay allowed me to end up in service to Mouron. He was looking for a willing spirit and I needed someone to save me from my fate, to guide and teach me, which Mouron has done very well."

Forenk felt enough at ease with Zook to ask, "How did you die?"

"I fell," said Zook, "Into a deep chasm and off of a cliff."

"Pursued by many foes no doubt," said Forenk, on the brink of being enthusiastic.

"Not exactly," there was an embarrassed silence for a long moment, then Zook continued, "I tripped,over a tree root." "By the eight teats of Thegotta, the same thing happened to me, the tripping over a tree root, that is. That is how my adventure started," said Forenk. He thought back to when he had tripped over a tree root into the river while attempting to save Donoxa whom he had accidentally bumped into the water. Forenk wondered if the girls had set up the accident as a way of meeting him. The thought of them set off many images in his mind and he mentally brushed them aside so as not to be rude to his new friend.

The discussion between the two young men, one dead and one living, went on until Gerojef interrupted, addressing the only one of the two he could see, he said, "Forenk, Master Mouron is retiring for the evening, perhaps it is time for us to turn in as well."

44 To Battle at the Tower Door

After bidding Zook good night and picking up a large melting candle, Forenk walked up the winding stone steps inside the tower to the guest sleeping chamber. There he climbed into a straw-covered bunk and pulled a woolen blanket over himself. Gerojef arranged himself in another bunk. It was quiet except for the occasional animal, insect and wind sounds of the night outside the tower.

Forenk felt Great, he had new friends, his belly was full, and he was safe in a tower with a powerful wizard who was not intimidated by the witch. A shiver ran down his spine at the mere thought of the vile Drogana and he knew he would be facing her again. He consoled himself with the confidence of Mouron who seemed optimistic about the outcome of this affair. He felt hopeful, more alive, even happier than he had ever felt in his life, except for the nights with the girls that first week, and that one time with Mormoomi and then right after that with the sea nymphs. Yes, he felt better than he ever had in his whole life except for those times.

The familiar sound of Gerojef's snoring filled the room but Forenk was so very tired. It had been a long day and so he just ignored the buzzing drone. Forenk wondered if Heela and Donoxa would visit him in his dreams again. His eyes closed of their own accord and he swiftly descended into a deep sleep.

Soon dreaming, Forenk walked alone in a wilderness much like the one that he and his traveling companions had crossed in their travels to Swine Mountain. Then he floated over hills and a sea of grass that turned to prairie scrubland that stretched out before him as he flew over it. The distant horizons were indistinct and the sky was filled with dense grayish clouds. Raindrops began to plop unto his neck and hands.

There was no sound, only a hollow feeling and awareness of being in a dream. He sensed danger nearby but he made no move to save himself or prepare to face it. Then he saw Donoxa and Heela. They waved to him from a distance but made no effort to join him but only looked back impassively. A voice like Mouron's said something in a warning tone. Forenk wondered why wizard was here with Donoxa and Heela on a journey. The dangers that existed in the waking world flooded back into his mind and he began to surface from the depths of the dream he remembered he was in. He sat up in bed.

Mouron called from the stone stairway. Dressed only in a night shirt, he said in a loud warning whisper, "Forenk, awaken, Gerojef, rise up, enemies are upon us!" When Mouron was sure they were both awake and rising, the wizard turned and returned down the stairs casting long eerie shadows from the torch he held before him. Mouron called out over his shoulder, "Quickly now, dress, we are in great peril!"

As if to corroborate the wizard's words the sounds of many footsteps and malicious voices came from outside beneath the window. Mixed with the harsh men's voices was the baying of beasts.

45 Agents of Goddess of Vengeance

Forenk quickly slipped on his pigskin boots and tied his pig intestine belt, anxiously adjusted the sheath of the Squirrel Sword, then stepped over to the table that held the candle but found no way to light it. He called softly, "Gerojef, can you see?"

In addition to the pale moonlight streaming in, there was some flickering lights coming in through the window from many torches outside.

Gerojef rustled aside a blanket as he stood up from his bunk. He said, "I see enough to know we must not tarry," as he slipped on his sandals and grabbed his staff.

Watching the steps as carefully as they could while rushing down the curved stairway they found Mouron by the door, adjusting his robe by torchlight and listening to the growing din outside.

A strange voice called from outside, "Mouron! Open up and allow us to enter, we are travelers in need of shelter and food." The caller's voice barely disguised his condescension and belligerence.

Mouron answered, "Who is it that brings hunting beasts to my tower so untimely?" When the answer was slow in coming, Mouron said, "I'll not admit a strange mob in the middle of the night." With no pretense of sympathy the wizard said, "Begone!"

They could hear the speaker outside silencing the gang and someone struck or kicked one of the baying animals causing it to whimper. When the skittish throng had settled down a bit, the speaker outside used a subtler tone of voice, "My name is Notgoot. We travel to the sea to trade and set out late in the day. We are not strangers, but tribesmen and neighbors from the ruins two days west. Traders from our tribe often bring you trade goods!"

"Yes, but they come in broad day light and are

welcomed! But you, Notgoot, are here on a fell errand. If it is camp you seek, seek it elsewhere on your way to the sea and when you encamp, make it far from here. Now go!"

There was a long hushed moment.

"Please, we are without food." The voice outside the door made one last attempt at subterfuge.

When there was no reply, Notgoot growled and spat noisily then said, "Drogana, the Goddess of Vengeance, has commanded us to bring the boy-man with the sword back to our village. Throw him out the window and we will leave you be!"

"Villain!" cursed Mouron.

Forenk heard a sudden thud from a blow to the door and another curse as Mouron jumped back. The iron bands on the door rattled and the blade edge of an axe could be seen protruding through the dark wood.

Notgoot reviled from just outside the door, "We will camp inside your tower this night, wizard, and eat your innards for our meal."

Mouron began to rummage through the shelves lining the walls, collecting bottles and powders, while Notgoot ranted outside. Gerojef held his hands towards the dirt floor in front of the door and started an incantation.

Forenk nearly jumped out of his skin in surprise when Zook said, "One of the watch-wards I set alerted me to danger and I woke Mouron. He was right, Drogana has set the tribesmen upon you."

Notgoot yelled at the door, "We seek the piglander Forenk. He must be punished for offense against the goddess." The axe slammed into the door again while a score of guttural voices chanted encouragement and the baying beasts howled.

A jagged piece of door flew across the room splintered by the frame-rattling blows on the other side. The door was beginning to give way to the great axe that was being driven into it.

"I can not seem to locate a thing," whined Mouron. Forenk turned from the door for a moment to see the wizard in a cloud of billowed powder that he had spilled by accident when he used too much force to open a small black box.

"Oh, no, what was it?" The enchanter cried in bewilderment.

The door rang with another blow and a large splinter from the door slashed across Forenk's cheek, opening a long wound. One of the metal bands binding the door planks together clanged to the floor and Forenk could see waving torches through a large hole in the door.

"I must do something," said Zook somewhere near Forenk and he could feel the spirit familiar moving towards the door and then through it.

Zook bravery moved Forenk to action. He pulled the sword from the sheath and immediately a warm power flowed from the pommel to his wrist and radiated up his arm. He felt a link with the sword. He put his other hand on the sword and held it like a great club. A bastard sword, he remembered Heela telling him what type of sword it was. I will use it on some bastards tonight, Forenk thought to himself.

The door buckled and collapsed and through the opened portal Forenk saw a barbarian scream and run off waving his arms hysterically, jumping and yelping as if he were beset by stinging insects. Forenk thought he could hear Zook laughing.

A weird little bone-thin man, nude, although it was cold, and covered in blue and red dyes and darker rune tattoos, stepped forth from the throng of tribesmen. He carried a twisted staff adorned with animal pelts and feathers and as he held it aloft he screamed at the others to attack.

Mouron still searching for some missing ingredient, glanced through the door and spied the funny looking man with the blue and red color patterns on his naked body and muttered, "That must be the tribesmen's shaman."

The tribesmen dog-handlers issued attack commands to the hounds, a gang of large and vicious-looking black mastiffs, that had until then strained at the leash. They charged the door in unison with bared yellow fangs.

But even before they reached the doorway, up from the ground sprung up a man-shaped being of rock and soil. It was a gnome, an earth spirit summonsed by Gerojef who, exhausted from his efforts, collapsed to the side of the door.

The summoned earth elemental's arms sprouted tree limbs and roots which it used as tentacles to grab the hounds as they danced around the gnome trying to find a place to bite into. The gnome captured an armful of squirming hounds this way while blocking the door to the tower with its bulk.

The dogs growled and whined in panic as the gnome's rock encrusted arms crushed the bones and organs of their bodies. They snapped slavering jaws at the earth spirit's material body, only to come away with mouthfuls of crumbling pebbles and dirt. One of the dogs managed to jump free before it was crippled and pounced back and forth before the huge gnome, biting into its legs to no avail.

The shaman stepped forward another hands breath from the mob. He held his staff above his head. Turning his face up to the heavens, to the earth and in every direction, he called out in a language that reminded Forenk of the language Gerojef and Donoxa used when casting spells.

"The shaman, he is trying to dispel my earth elemental." croaked Gerojef, "Stop him!"

Without hesitation, Forenk attempted to squeeze past the gnome to get outside and at the shaman, but the shaman adroitly cast a spell that dispelled spirits before Forenk could work himself by the gnome. Suddenly the earth spirit's body of soil and rock sank into the ground amid a puff of red smoke even as Forenk got outside the door. The shaman had succeeded and dispelled the earth spirit from the material plane.

Forenk's momentum carried him outside where he hopped over the bodies of the crushed mastiffs. Then he stood alone, surrounded on three sides by a score of armed men and vicious hounds. There was dead silence for a long moment as the throng of murderers assessed this new threat. He looked one of the men in the eye and the fellow's eyes widened in terror as if Forenk were a menace. One of the remaining dogs shrank back, slinking behind its handler master.

Another tribesman, arms swinging akimbo at something

no one else could see, broke from the circle and ran into the night. Forenk thought he heard Zook laugh again.

The shaman rubbed a tattoo on his arm and blue light leapt out. Forenk heard Zook howl in mournful pain.The shaman, grimacing evilly from a blue-tattooed face, madness in his eyes, having disposed of Zook and an earth elemental, stared with defiance at Forenk.

There was a sound of breaking pottery from within the tower causing everyone to start. Forenk heard Mouron stammering apologetically at his clumsiness as the mob of tribesmen and dogs advanced towards Forenk, their awe of him waning. Notgoot, on direction from the shaman, cried, "This is the one! Take his sword and kill him!"

A mastiff as large as a pony growled as it sprang at Forenk, forcing him to use the sword. The dog landed in a pile at Forenk's feet, the top half of the canine's head sailed into the crowd with a wet slap and cries of disgust came from the mob as they back-stepped hastily. The second dog sniffed the air and barked at Forenk and back tracked behind one of the tribesmen.

The largest of the tribesmen wearing a brown and gray beast's skin, his one article of clothing, stepped forward and said in a language that Forenk had trouble understanding, "I am Notgoot, war chief of my tribe and we are here because the Goddess of Vengeance has ordered us to bring the sword to her. We will not return to the Goddess without the sword."

"If this goddess you speak of receives the dead, then you may be returning to her very soon," said Forenk, hardly believing that those words had come from his mouth.

Frightened, Notgoot stared at Forenk as if he believed him, then bit-by-bit regained his composure. He turned to his men and cried, "Fellow warriors, my tribesmen, we are many and our enemy is one. Although he holds a sacred weapon and is god spawn, Drogana tells us his spirit will not seek vengeance on us. His body is mortal and his flesh can be injured, see how he bleeds!" Notgoot pointed to Forenk's cheek seeping blood and a hubbub arose as the men saw proof of his vulnerability.

"We will rush the sword bearer together. A few of us may die but we will slay him and return to our goddess in victory. What say you all?" The shouts of consent were half hearted but the tribesmen shook the spears and axes they carried.

"Wait!" commanded the shaman. He smiled manically and said, "I will call a spirit to blind him first and spare the sons of our village." With that the shaman raised his arms dramatically and started the summons in a weird otherworldly voice.

Forenk jumped forward and swung the sword towards the shaman, who stumbled backwards shrieking. Only the tip of the sword reached its mark but even so it bit halfway through the shaman's arm. The miniature geyser of red blood that spurted out of the shaman's arm splattered the blue tattoos all over his body. The shaman screamed once and then fell backwards. A couple of tribesmen leapt to aid the shaman. Notgoot, armed with a wicked looking two-handed battle axe attempted to sneak up behind Forenk while the others held him occupied and at bay.

Knowing his life depended on it, Forenk swung the Squirrel Sword and the blade bit deeply into Notgoot's side.

Frozen for a flash, Notgoot coughed, blood bubbling out of his mouth, then he toppled over with a look of disbelief on his brutal face. Forenk, the divine sword as light as air in his hand, pulled the sword from Notgoot's body in time to block and parry axes swung by the swart hairy tribesmen men rushing him while he was distracted. The next swing of the Squirrel Sword cut across a pair of assassins, hewing through leather armor and opening up the flesh to the bone.

Forenk's sword split, severed and sundered the flesh of the tribesmen. For one golden instant Forenk was exultant, awash in blood, alive in the experience, seeing through the eyes of the hero. This legendary vision quickly dissolved and was replaced by his revulsion as globules of warm still-living gore splattered his face and the screams of agony from the men he was butchering pierced his ears.

Forenk was grateful it ended quickly when half of the

attackers still standing broke and ran. The other half, about a dozen men, lay dead, dying or severely wounded, a few sobbed and moaned. Standing there, looking over the carnage, covered in the viscous gore of the tribesmen, Forenk suddenly felt acutely nauseous and could not help but empty his stomach where he stood.

46 Zook Over Yonder

Shortly afterwards, Mouron and Gerojef came out to minister to the injured tribesmen, although Gerojef did so only with hesitation. But he was generous with his admiration of Forenk.

"You did it, Forenk. You defeated Drogana's lackeys in true hero style," said the old Druid. "And saved our lives, I am dreadfully sorry for my muddle of things before, I daresay I almost caused things to go worse." Mouron said.

"No, you did fine, you stood up to them. None of it was your fault, they would not have come if not for me," said Forenk.

Mouron said, "Well, in any event, you certainly sorted things out for the time being, dreadful business. Hmm."

"It was the sword really did it all," Forenk answered the wizard, glumly embarrassed by so much positive attention.

"No, Forenk, the properties of the sword may have helped, but you behaved most bravely," said Mouron.

Forenk was studying the ground then looked up and said, "I don't like killing men. What will happen to me?"

"You had no choice Forenk, you will not be blamed or held accountable by any law, except for Drogana's, for defending yourself."

"Drogana's law?" asked Forenk.

"What about Drogana's law? Yes, I meant in her eyes you are guilty by association. You have the sword that she believes should be hers. It is a relic of great symbolic power. You need not be concerned with any laws of hers, except that she is powerful in this land. You are the living embodiment of the conquerer that has lessened her power and prestige here. As you have seen she has followers like the Tribesmen of the Ruins and divine powers of her own. There are rumors of why she is worshipped as the goddess of vengeance. She has become a malignant, spiteful witch goddess who curses all who offer her even the slightest wrong."

Forenk nodded, understanding. He said, "And I have offered great wrong in her thinking." He looked around and said, "Where is Zook? Is he all right?

"That is a mystery. I fear the shaman may have bound him. We will delve into the matter at first light," answered Mouron.

Forenk slept the last few hours of the night and rose to find Mouron awake and down in the galley kitchen. Mouron explained to Forenk that he had cast locate spell attuned to zook and had discovered that the Shaman of the Tribesmen of the Ruins had used a spirit trapping spell to bind Zook to one of his tattoo spell runes. Mouron explained that a spirit binding spell could be used to magically place a spirit under the control of a spell caster.

"That's what's been used to capture our friend Zook I fear. They may attempt to control him, but I expect they will destroy him by draining his energy for some other purpose," said Mouron.

"Are you sure? How can we free him?" asked Forenk hopefully.

"As you may have noted," said the wizard, "I am not at my best under duress. But detecting magic has always come naturally to me, if such a thing is possible." Mouron waited for Forenk's concurrence and then continued, "The Shaman knew, more than likely with Drogana's help, that I had a spirit familiar. He came prepared. His staff had magic runes upon it. I went looking for something to nullify the rune spells but can't remember what that is right now, but the point is…." A look of bewilderment crept across the wizard's face.

"Something about the spirit magic?" said Forenk.

Mouron said, "Yes, thats it, creating the binding spell is a lengthy ritual. The same for Gerojef's summoned earth elemental, that shaman dispelled it so easily, with virtually no preparation. Very powerful magic, more than I would think possible for the Shaman of a small remote tribe. This is Drogana's power in play, of that I have no doubt."

"If Zook is in danger, we must rescue him," said Forenk.

The sun was peeped over the trees on the horizon as Mouron turned and smiled at Forenk in admiration and said, "I was thinking it may prove too dangerous or be too late. But if there is a chance, then we must do what is necessary."

"He is my friend and I must try. But you have not slept. Perhaps it would be better if you stayed here and looked after these wounded men and Gerojef."

The old Druid was sleeping, having slipped into a fever after helping patch up the battle-wounded men. After some debate, Forenk and Mouron decided that Forenk would go on his own. Mouron insisted on furnishing provisions, a water bottle and enough food for four days, in a backpack.

Mouron looked Forenk over and said, "The Tribesmen of the Ruins fear you and I wager you will cause much trepidation, but act quickly, show no mercy, for they will slay you if given the chance. If Zook has not been destroyed, free him from my service. He may do what he will and go where he will. You may tell him so."

The enchanter rubbed his eyes sleepily, looking in the direction the party of marauders had gone. He said, "Unless they marched without sleeping, which frightened men may do, they will not be far ahead. Surprise is our ally. Hurry Forenk, and, may the gods smile on you."

With that sentiment lingering in his thoughts, Forenk, son of the Goddess of Pigland, slipped into the woods in the direction of the ruins.

47 Mud and Blood

Forenk had acquired some minor hunting skills while trapping in the woods around Pig Whistle. Kormed, his adoptive father had taken Forenk hunting many times and so even as an aging boy he was able to go out and set small game traps unaided.

On one occasion a vicious pig-eating bandersnatch had haunted the woods of Pig Whistle and terrorized the pig farmers by making off with their hogs and an occasional villager. The men of the village went out into the night armed with axe, pitchfork, bow and arrows smeared in poisonous pig poop. Forenk had come along, as had several of the young villagers, to hold the torches for the men as they trailed the beast through the dark, stealthily following a trail of disturbed foliage.

They came upon the beast feeding. The bandersnatch was as large as two men put together and half as tall again, with giant-sized eagle like talons, but even so, it was still no match for a mob of armed men. Forenk recalled the screechy bellow of the monster as the men cornered it near the river where it refused to relinquish it's meal, a fattened pig. The men, in spite of the incompetence they experienced when Forenk was around, attacked the beast almost as one, and after receiving no more than a few lacerations, the men slew the bandersnatch. He saw the body in the torchlight, twice the size of a man, scales and fur. A strange sour smell issued from the corpse.

The village of Pig Whistle, as was custom, celebrated for a week afterwards and the slayers of the beast, they had overwhelmed a dumb foe by sheer numbers, were treated as heroes until the next threat came about. Forenk thought of that time as he strode along following the easily visible track of footprints that the fleeing tribesmen left in their wake.

Forenk's enemies had out numbered him more than a score to one. That was the size of the mob of villagers that had attacked the bandersnatch. He came with in a hair's breadth of realizing the simple irony. Instead he thought to himself, perhaps I am a hero for only a hero could perform such feats as I have.

Forenk stopped. He had let himself become over-confidant in his thinking again. He remembered the consequences of that foolishness. He remembered the aid and leadership his allies had given him and he remembered the Squirrel Sword. He wondered how he would have fared against the vicious killers sent by Drogana without the magical weapon. He put his mind back to minding the trail of the tribesmen.

Forenk had moved fast and followed the fresh spoor for half a day. He figured that the Tribesmen of the Ruins, several of them wounded, among them the shaman, could not be moving that fast and could not have been much further ahead. He pushed on, treading through the thickening forest. Mouron had told him that the ruins were on the outskirts of a forest that the tribesmen, incapable of imagination, had named The Forest.

A little while later in the day Forenk saw an squirrel in a nearby tree and almost choked. This squirrel had a tail and was not the tiny but dreadful monster who had haunted his trail those long torturous days. Even with his newfound confidence and abilities, the thought of the little horror sent a feverish chill through him. The squirrel squeak-barked at him distracting him for a moment. When he looked back at the trail and noticed that the track he had been following had split up, but it was too late to avoid the ambush.

He felt a sharp pain in his neck and saw, out of the corner of his eye, an arrow protruding from where the pain now pulsed. It seemed to just appear there, as if by magic, but then several arrows whizzed towards him and turning he saw the tribesmen armed with bows stepping out of hiding places. A jolt of pain wracked his body. The arrow had gone deep and turning his neck ripped material in the flesh.

The bowmen watched Forenk nervously lest he surprise them once again with his ruinous attack but continued to notch their bows and fired again. Even at point blank range a few of the projectiles missed, but one arrow hit Forenk in the side and another in the leg.

Forenk managed to draw the Squirrel Sword but began to lose control of his body and then toppled over. He dropped the sword. The gang of tribesmen were on him like frightened animals. They first grabbed the sword and then began to kick and beat Forenk's bleeding and nearly unconscious form. Forenk had initially felt the pain of the arrows but sank into into shock mostly oblivious to the beating he took.

The Shaman of the ruins, the stump of his left arm in a bloody bandage, limped into the clearing. He ordered the tribesmen to back away from Forenk. Forenk looked up through a haze to the shaman's contorted face. Half conscious, in shock and longing to slip into a deep sleep Forenk knew he had to stay awake for any chance of survival. He felt the backpack digging into his back, they had not taken it, only the sword.

The shaman was standing there talking it seemed to himself but then he heard a familiar woman's voice. The voice was in his head, like Zook's had been. It was Drogana and she said, "Tell them to tie his hands."

Forenk wondered dreamily why they would bother tying his hands, he felt the life slipping out of him, he could barely stay conscious. He thought that he would soon be dead.

"Tie his hands to that tree," said the Shaman to a couple of tribesmen standing nearby. Two tribesmen dragged him roughly to the tree. Multiple pangs of pain shot through Forenk's body causing him to moan out loud as they tied his hands behind him to the bole of the tree.

Forenk looked up into the crazed eyes of the Shaman, The shaman held up his arm stump and said in a voice that reminded Forenk of a snake's hiss, "The goddess is here with me and she wishes for you to pay for the injuries you inflicted."

"Leave him there, the Ancestor Squirrel will finish him!" said the voice that was Drogana's although she could not be seen.

Forenk realized she was in spirit form, he had destroyed her physical body, and he could hear her just like he had been able to hear Zook. That reminded him of his mission to save his new friend and so he called out with his mind like he had learned to do, "Zook, Zook, are you there?"

"Well, you are full of surprises, Forenk, spirit talker!" It was Drogana who answered him. She said, "Was the wizard's familiar a friend of yours? He will serve us from now on." She laughed, was silent for a moment and then with venom in her words she said, "I told you I would be back for my revenge! bastard mortal! I will eat your soul when the squirrel is finished eating what is left of your manhood. Hee, hee heeeeee. I will be reborn as ruler of these lands and your little Pigland, too."

The shaman kicked at Forenk but he could hardly feel the blow. The shaman spit at him and then backed away cursing Forenk and making signs to ward off Forenk's ghost with his good arm just in case Forenk decided to haunt him from the grave.

Drogana said, "I will take great pleasure in slaying your mother, the Sow Goddess, and Jykee will be revenged! And you will be the greatest part of my revenge on your mighty father, the Mud God. No more will his progeny walk the world! He will suffer my long waited revenge!"

Drogana howled like an animal and said, "Mipinus invaded these lands. They were mine! My husband Jykee's land!" Her voice seethed with anger and madness. She said, "Enough, come away shaman, I waste my time with the offspring of mud and swine."

As they left Forenk heard Drogana address the shaman, "Will you be able to perform the ceremony with one arm, servant?"

"Yes, Goddess," the shaman replied, " A surprise guest for the Piglander's sow mother!"

They both laughed and then left the clearing and Forenk was alone. He wondered how things could possibly have changed so drastically, gone so wrong, so quickly and unexpectedly. He had bested the witch, beaten the tribesmen in battle. He had been pursuing them to rescue Zook. But now the quest had failed and many of his friends had died on his behalf. Forenk wondered if maybe he deserved to die, he had caused so many problems.

The sky had become gray while he lay there straining to stay conscious. Drops of rain began to fall from the heavens. The rain increased and Forenk could feel the ground absorbing the water. It seeped into his bloody breeches.

Although he felt weak with the life ebbing out of him, Forenk opened his eyes one more time. His head rested awkwardly against the bole of the tree, his hands tied over his head and around the tree. He could see the arrows sticking out of his body and mats of blood in his clothes grew as he watched.

Then there was something else. It was a small animal, a squirrel with a small stump for a tail, coming towards his helpless body. The Ancestor Squirrel from the sacred grove the same one who had bitten off one of Forenk's testicles and left him terrified and sleepless.

Now, when Forenk could do nothing to protect him self as the furry horror stopped at Forenk's feet and smiled wickedly at him. Then it leapt onto Forenk's knee and casually hopped towards his groin.

Frantic, somehow Forenk recalled a spell of changing. Mumbling the magic words, the rope that held his hands tied around the tree metamorphosed into a serpent. The serpent sprang at the squirrel, coiling its clammy body around the wet fur of the squirrel. The squirrel's eyes bulged as the serpent constricted. The snake bit into the squirrels head with a mouth full of fangs.

Just as suddenly the snake turned back into a rope which fell harmlessly to the ground. The squirrel thumped to the ground and tried to crawl away, its body contorted with broken bones. With the last of his strength Forenk grabbed the squirrel and crushed the squirrel's head in his bare hands until he could feel the tiny bones collapse.

He tossed the small corpse aside. Too weak to feel vindicated, he coughed up blood and winced in pain from the effort. Completely overwhelmed by the ordeal he had gone through Forenk passed out.

48 Memus

"Forenk," said Donoxa.

"Open your eyes," said Heela. Forenk opened his eyes. He was lying on his back and he leaned up on one arm to see before him his former companions, naked, immaculate and more radiant than ever.

He looked around to find he was still in the forest where he had closed his eyes in death sleep, but he also felt as if he were far away at the same time. The scene was resting on a cloudy mist that blurred the distance and somehow seemed more substantial than the woods which now seemed to be insubstantial and illusory. The pain of his wounds were gone, as were the arrows.

"Heela, Donoxa, it is so good to see you," Forenk tried to hold back the tears that streamed down his face streaking dirt and drying blood. "Am I dead?" he asked.

"No Forenk, you would have died but you have brought yourself here to Memus, the home of the gods," said Heela. "but It is not time for you to leave the world. You have much to do before you join the gods."

"I'm not dead," said Forenk, pronounced equally as a question and a statement. "Where are we, it looks somewhat ike the woods where I was ambushed but not so at the same time. Wait, you said I brought myself here?"

The two angelic nymphs spoke as one, their voices resonating like a song's echo. They said, "Memus touches the world past the veil of mortality. It is everywhere conjoined with the world of flesh and blood lying boundary-less within the fabric of the celestial cosmos. You have touched with your spirit senses the world past the veil of mortality and brought yourself by sheer will to the home of the gods."

Then Donoxa spoke alone, "Memus, the home of the gods is like a layer of fabric of the celestial cosmos and lies within and without the material world, so you are still in that forest but also here with us in Memus."

Forenk tried to get his mind to understand what they were saying, but deep inside he knew and believed their words to be true. He felt like the old Forenk, the pig farmer, was running to keep up with the new version of himself, the son of gods. He was aware of a force running through him like a flood of liquid light. The stiffness left his joints and was replaced by the impression of buoyancy.

"What will we do now?" asked Forenk.

"You must use your intuition, what does your heart tell you?" Asked Heela.

Forenk thought of Drogana's threat to kill the Goddess of Pigland, his mother. "I need to get back to my village, Drogana has threatened my mother. And the sword, they took it, I will need it to fulfill the prophecy!" he said.

Forenk started to rise but as he did so he noticed a form loom up, materialize out of the haze behind Heela and Donoxa. The tall figure had pale white skin that shone in contrast to her night black robes.

"Drogana!" shouted Forenk.

Her magical disguise was more diabolically glorious than ever. She was more beautiful than any of the agents of the divine that Forenk had seen and Forenk was momentarily hypnotized by her grim but dazzling visage.

"I see you approve of my new body, the one I will wear as the new goddess of the woodland," said Drogana.

His guardians rose from Forenk's side to confront Drogana, but she lifted her hands and a blue radiance pulsed out of her palms. The blue substance that grew out of the witch goddess's hand cowed Heela and Donoxa. They struggled as the water-like energy engulfed them. Once they were completely encased, arms pressed against their sides, they could not move or speak.

"You have no power to stop me, I am a goddess, equal to your master." Drogana crackled, her disturbing screech betraying the perversity of her mind and the corruption hidden by the spell of glamour she had cast on herself.

She turned to Forenk and said, "Let us see you use your intuition to guess what will happen now." She looked at Forenk. Bereft of his sword he posed little threat. Still, Drogana's sardonic smile twisted into a malevolent snarl and she said, "The sight of you reminds me of my husband's humiliation, our loss of respect and homage, but I shall suffer that sight no longer!"

She slowly raised her hands, her mouth stretching open wide contorting her face into a hideous demon's.

"I told you I would eat your soul, prepare for soulless oblivion, spawn of the Mud God."

As if summonsed by the evocation of his name a booming voice issued from somewhere out of Forenk's field of vision. "Drogana, you are not equal to Mipinus and you will suffer sight no longer."

Drogana wailed pitifully, shaking her head, clutching at her face and screaming, "My eyes, my eyes, oh, I am undone!" She lifted her eyelids to reveal the black and empty spaces of her eye sockets.

The unseen voice of Mipinus boomed again, "Black-hearted witch! You have disturbed a covenant created by the gods. You show no gratitude for being raised in influence by your honorable husband, Jykee. It is known to him, how you contrived through the use of tainted magic to sway his heart and steal his power Know then witch, hence forth, you are no longer wife to Jykee."

Drogana moaned and spat, "I will still have my revenge! Even now my servants will… Aieeee!" Her tirade was interrupted by Mipinus's words as her body twisted and convulsed.

"Silence devil, even your very visage is an insult to the eye, hence forth you shall have no earthly body, as a spirit unable to possess form shall you wander through eternity."

Forenk witnessed her body resume the vile and bloated sac he had seen when he slew her former earthly body. She scuttled away crablike, shrinking, and then was gone.

Forenk heard Drogana's spirit speech. She whispered,

"Revenge!" Turning back to Mipinus, he saw the outline silhouetted by a white radiance that glowed from an unseen source behind.

The booming voice of Mipinus, now gentler, said, "Forenk, pig son, remember the rede that Mormoomi gave. You have a prophecy to fulfill."

Forenk wanted to ask questions, get a better look at Mipinus but the mists and Mipinus's hazy figure and even Donoxa and Heela, now free of Drogana's magic, began to fade away. Forenk wondered if he had been dreaming or maybe he really was dead.

49 To Wreak and Ruins

Forenk woke with a start back in the forest where he had lost consciousness. The tribesmen's arrows that had pierced his flesh and nearly slain him lay strewn to one side. Pain seemed to fall from him like dust. He felt renewed, exhilarated by escaping death. He remembered someone reminding him that he was mortal. Then he heard the voices of Mouron and Gerojef as they appeared carrying wood and other vegetation.

"Gerojef! Mouron! Well met!" Forenk shouted hoarsely. Not completely recovered, the effort caused him to wince.

"Amazing!" said Gerojef, his eyes bugging out at Forenk, "I thought we were going to lose him. You must give me the formula to that healing paste, Mouron."

The wizard smiled, "I will, hard to gather some of the ingredients, but as you can see, well worth the effort. Do not get up yet Forenk, give the healing salve time to do its work."

"Forenk, you were at death's door and banging on the door for entry, I might add!" said Gerojef. "I thought I would be saying farewell for good, my boy. Thanks be, praise to Mouron, the great!"

"Oh nonsense, I am a befuddled old man who occasionally remembers old tricks," said Mouron defensively, but could not help smiling, being well pleased with the compliment. "Rest Forenk, we will build a fire and and keep watch. In the morning you should be revived enough to help us retrieve the sword and fulfill your quest," he said.

"We will prepare a bit more medicine for you," said Gerojef, arranging some herbs and roots and then starting a fire. "You have suffered what came close to being a grave setback but have miraculously managed to be on the mend. Drogana will not be expecting you to hinder her plans any further," said the druid.

Forenk laid his head back on a blanket and stared up through the leaves and branches of the trees to see patches of stars in the heavens. The rains had stopped and the clouds had passed and Forenk saw a shooting star before he drifted off into a deep slumber.

A whistling bird's song woke Forenk. Mouron was at the fire preparing a meal and greeted Forenk when he noticed he had awoken. Gerojef snored loudly from the other side of the fire.

"Did you sleep well?" asked Mouron. "We will allow Gerojef a bit more sleep and then breakfast. Do you care for squirrel stew, I believe you mentioned something about it at some point, or was that me?"

An hour later they were preparing to break camp. "The ruined ruins are not more than a few hours forced march from here," said Mouron.

"I will get us there sooner!" Gerojef said. The druid had consumed some of the herbs that he and Mouron had gathered and had revived to his former energetic self. Gerojef held up a hand and spoke an evocation. When he finished, silence fell on the scene. Forenk began to ask Gerojef what they were expecting when the sound of riders fell on their ears.

"The tribesmen return!" said Forenk, rising to his feet.

"No," said Gerojef. "Aid rides to us to furnish the speed that necessity demands." Three large beasts burst into view and rode into the small clearing. They were giant antelope, with tremendous pointed horns and they snorted and dug at the ground as if impatient to proceed.

Gerojef spoke to the beasts in his strange druid's tongue and the beasts nodded their heads as if they understood. Gerojef told the somewhat alarmed Forenk and Mouron to mount the giant antelopes. "Hold on to the beast's mane, we will be traveling fast," said Gerojef. He whistled once and as the three steeds launched into a trot Gerojef broke into a druidic stave.

Beast of woodland riders of the wind
A boon I beg bring us to the villains den
To serve justice to set us fair
Ride my beauties faster than air

With Gerojef's words ringing in their ears, the three animals carrying the companions sprang forward into a dizzying gallop. Forenk held tight and duck as the large beast swerved, precariously avoiding low hanging tree branches, underfoot bush and fallen logs. So great was the speed they traveled that the wind sang as it pushed against Forenk's face.

Before long, the forest thinned out and the crumbling remains of stone architecture began to appear. Sporadically at first and then more frequently, larger remnants of structures came into view until entire building, burned out or crumbling could be seen. Stone and mortar building were strange to Forenk and they reminded him of the ones he had seen in Eysor.

In the shortening distance they saw a group of the tribesmen. As they sped onwards they could see the form of the one-armed shaman among them.

The shaman and tribesmen watched the riders approaching not sure what to make of them. By the time they recognized their mounted pursuers, they were upon them, scattering the tribesmen like leaves before a gale.

The shaman began to jabber a spell but Mouron cast a blue bolt of blinding jagged light from a wand that smashed into the tribal shaman, lifting him off his feet and carrying him many yards before dashing him to the ground. He rolled a good distance more before coming to a stop, where he lay still.

Forenk saw one of the tribesman carrying the Squirrel Sword and his mount instinctively turned and charged the running figure, who dropped the sword and ran away. Forenk made a heroic leap off the mount and grabbed the sword in a graceful movement and would have remounted on the run had he not tripped on an inconvenient chunk of masonry. Instead Forenk tumbled over in an uncoordinated and unflattering spasmodic cartwheel. He ended up sprawled awkwardly in a position that managed to renew the pain in every wound he had suffered.

Gerojef, rode up beside him and seeing he was getting up on his own, said smiling, "Still a bit clumsy I see."

50 Swine Marches On

After the last of the tribesmen had run off, Mouron examined the tribal shaman's body and was able to free Zook by dispelling the enchantment binding the spirit to a rune tattoo. After a brief reconciliation, Mouron said, "Zook, for your loyal and courageous service you are free to take a leave of absence, to go on your way, if that is what you desire. You will not have to pass on to the gray spirit lands until you are ready."

Forenk could hear Zook replying, "Thank you Master Mouron, I suppose I could return home for a visit and there is still much to see in the world. I shall return after a look at what is beyond." Zook then spoke directly to Forenk, "Until we meet again Forenk, my friend, for I feel we will."

Forenk said his goodbyes and watched through the magic mirror, that had some how survived the ordeal tucked in his backpack, as his new friend faded from view.

Meanwhile, Gerojef spotted a particularly slow witted tribesman who was unsuccessfully hiding behind the wrong side of a pillar. Questioning him they discovered that Drogana had returned to her followers at the ruins after being blinded by Mipinus. They learned that by barging in when they had they had managed to foul the ritual making the sword the official emblem of Drogana's sovereignty.

However, before they had arrived and in a final attempt to revenge herself on Forenk, Drogana had summoned a malkaloki, an evil and sadistic trickster demon. This offspring of the chaos devil had been sent to Pig Whistle, Forenk's home village, to wreak vengeance in Drogana's behalf.

After they had gotten all the information they deemed important, Gerojef pointed to the frightened tribesman and asked, "What shall we do with this barbarian?"

"Let him go. His people are the dregs of an ancient empire whose most notable characteristic was the immediate subjugation and enslavement of any beings they came in contact with. This is the capitol, Kankehsor, and as you can see, their descendants, the current residents, are a miserable lot. But we at least can be charitable," said Mouron.

"You can go," commanded Gerojef, untying the captive's bindings. When the tribesman got up and immediately made to run, Gerojef put out his foot and tripped him.

"Oops!" said Gerojef, as the tribesman scrambled up and got his footing. The tribesman began to stagger off when Gerojef swung his leg back and kicked hard, planting a foot strategically as to give the surviving tribesman momentum in the direction he was headed. They all watched him disappear deeper in to the ruins of what once must have been a large city.

Forenk said, "I hope he will be alright, but I must speed to Pig Whistle, my home village, to save my mother from the malkaloki demon." He held the sword up dramatically and said, "As the prophecy says 'Home of the Squirrel Sword is the swine!'"

"Did one of those arrows hit your skull by any chance?" asked Gerojef, "The second part of Mormoomi's oracle was, if I remember correctly, 'sword of the squirrel home to the swine.' But you are right, the time has come to bring the Sacred Squirrel Sword to the swine, that would be Pigland, or, no offense, your mother, the Goddess of Pigland."

51 Swine Waits for No One

Forenk expressed his gratitude to Mouron for re-enchanting, or more accurately removing the spells that dampened, the divine power of the Squirrel Sword. "I would have failed without the sword's power restored. And what ever challenges lay ahead I will be able to face knowing I am armed to meet them," said Forenk.

"It was my honor to take part in your divine quest. You have done the world a great service by defeating Drogana. She was determined to bring these lands under her control, and without her husband Jykee, known for his general benevolence, a tyrannical queendom it would have been. Jykee was fair minded and I think Drogana seduced him to gain the power of a queen of the gods," said Mouron.

After bidding Mouron farewell, Forenk and Gerojef mounted the giant antelope and began the long trek back to the Sty River. They took the overland route, traveling at many times the speed they had first covered on their way north to Swine Mountain and Mouron's Tower.

They stopped at Swine Mountain to inform Hezfytis of their progress and their destination. Hezfytis approved of their plan and after an over night rest they were off at first light.

They continued over rugged rocky hills and through scrubby shrubbery. Directing the swift mounts on a direct path to a ford north of Pig Whistle. While they were crossing the shallow river in the hills above Pig Whistle, Forenk thought he heard his name called and reined in the giant antelope he rode by pulling back on its black mane.

"Beware Forenk, the squirrels are upon us!" The dual voices of Heela and Donoxa, voices he had come to love, sounded in Forenk's head in eerie echoes. "We came to Pig Whistle to aid you in completing your quest but have been captured by Drogana's summonsed malkaloki."

Forenk heard what sounded like a moan of pain or maybe

of sensual pleasure and as it faded he called, "Wait, does mother live?" His glorious guardians did not respond.

"Are you speaking with the spirits again?" asked Gerojef, reining in the giant stomping antelope he sat upon by pulling back desperately on its thick black mane.

"Donoxa and Heela have somehow returned but have been captured by one of Drogana's demons!" said Forenk. He repeated the warning the women had given him.

Gerojef said, "I know of the malkaloki. They are champion demons, captains among devils, deadly tricksters and very powerful both with arms and mystical powers. You will have a real test of your new skills if we shall meet one of them."

"Yes but we must hurry before it is too late to save mother and the women," pleaded Forenk.

Gerojef commanded the woodland mounts to speedy effort. Forenk could feel the wind push against his face as the magical beast he virtually flew through a landscape that passed so fast that is became blurred.

The sun began to set as they gained the approaches to the village of Pig Whistle, Forenk's home. As they rode up to the outlying farms on the fringe of the village they smelled smoke and saw flames in the distance. Tiny figures zig-zagged helter-skelter around the farmstead fields and buildings while hog squeals mingled with pig farmer screams and hollers. Forenk realized with horror that the small darting shapes were squirrels.

52 A Swine to Kill, A Swine to Squeal

Townsfolk, assaulted by hordes of the small squirrel marauders, ran while they screamed, swatted themselves to dislodge furry attackers. Helpless pigs covered by patches of possessed squirrels, squealed and spun in circles, turned and bit back when they could at the rodent riders. Everywhere there was carnage, fires burned at the few wooden cottages and combustible thatch roofs. The mud and waddle huts did not burn as well but blackened and fumed cinders and black smoke from the corners and openings.

Forenk dismayed by the sorry sight that greeted him gritted his teeth. A powerful pang of emotion, much like what he felt when he had skewered Drogana to the tree, surged through him. He drew the Squirrel Sword free of it's tattered scabbard and it shone in the dimming sunset.

Using the weapon from the back of the giant antelope proved difficult, for the diminutive prey dodged quickly, many of his deft sword swings missed the mark. Forenk leapt to the ground while the beast was still in a trot, and where Forenk would have ungainly tumbled and landed in an aching and bruised fetal position in the past, now he only lost his balance and stumbled, giving his hands and knees a mild skinning.

From the ground Forenk could see Gerojef was likewise at a loss as to the best offense and prodded his mount this way and that, chasing off which ever squirrel happened to be nearest. As Forenk rose to his feet, a young woman being chased by a particularly ferocious looking squirrel ran towards him. She squealed for help and practically jumped into his arms. Forenk managed to catch her with one arm and swing the sword with the other, neatly slicing the squirrel in half. The girl turned to him and the elated approval on her face changed to surprise and puzzlement.

"Forenk, Is that really you?" she said, "Your back and what a big sword you have!"

Recognition dawned on Forenk. The young woman was Floexa, the chieftain's eldest daughter and the fairest maiden of the village. She smelled of pig excrement and in comparison with the females Forenk had grown accustomed to in his recent adventures she was unpleasant to behold.

"Errm, uh, yes. I am back and, and there is work to be done," said Forenk. He gently shoved her aside and turned towards the center of squirrel chaos that his home village had been engulfed in. Forenk strode into the mad melee rescuing surviving villagers he came upon. He only swung the sword a few times at the larger more aggressive squirrel champions because most kept clear of the blade that left a trail of headless and sundered squirrel corpses.

Elsewhere, anywhere Forenk had not sliced a swath of squirrel death through, the malevolent rodent rampage remained. Squirrels terrorized the village, hopping to and fro, nipping at screaming children and the elderly. A few hardy folk had died defending the village or were too slow to get away as fast as the majority of villagers that had run off at the first sign of the squirrel attack.

Forenk could see that hordes of Drogana's murderous minions continued to pillage and raze the village. He made his way through the bedlam slicing into the uncharacteristically ferocious fur-covered marauders. Making his way to his home Forenk saw the flames first. His family's hut was burned to smoking ashes, some remnants of the wattle walls bore stubborn flames.

Forenk surprised and executed a squirrel who stood near the still blazing husk of the abode holding an incriminating burning twig. A look of shock replaced the amusement on it's tiny rodent's buck-toothed visage as the head parted from the body and sailed into the flames.

Kormed lay in muck of the pig pen, blood seeped from dozens of squirrel bites and scratches.

"Father!" bawled Forenk, running to and propping the old man up against his knee.

"I am fine, I tripped getting out of the house, chasing one

of those damn varmints!" said Kormed. He looked up and a smile animated his normally expressionless features. "Frink. my boy, you haven't been eaten by these damn squirrels yet, thats good." He glanced at the Squirrel Sword and said, "Whew, that is a beauty, nice sword, where did you manage to get it?"

"My name is Forenk, father, and I have returned from a great quest," said Forenk.

"You were gone?" asked his father.

"Err , yes father, it's been over a month I think."

"I was wondering just the other day why you had not been doing your chores, and now that I think about it, your mother kept talking about you and great deeds, I did not pay much heed. Too bad about her, that monster killed her about an hour ago," said Kormed, his smile replaced by a look of grief.

"Killed her? Monster, what monster? When, what happened?"
whined Forenk, swinging the sword back handed and disemboweling a squirrel that thought he could bite Forenk while he had his back turned.

"The one with all the horns on top of his head, down by Hetman Walla's hut with two young gals. Those gals were something, I have not seen girls like that since we chased some bathers out of town a while back," said Kormed.

Storing this last bit of information away, Forenk turned and ran toward the chieftain's hut. Out of necessity he ignored the general helter-skelter of ravaging rodents, fires and the wails of the assaulted.

The thatch roof of the chieftain's hut had been burned away, burning charcoal cinders littered the dirt floor. One of the stone walls had collapsed and racing up, Forenk turned the corner of the rubble wall and was greeted by a wickedly tall figure armed with a large whip. Long pointed horns ran from side to side in a row protruding from a head topping off a muscular looking physique. The demon's skin was gray and had patches of yellow and red and it was clearly male.

The demigod devil turned its evil face towards Forenk.

The Malkaloki

53 The Swine Divine

The malkaloki wore nothing but a menacing grin on his devil face, but a glimmer of doubt crossed his inhuman features when he saw the Squirrel Sword in Forenk's hand.

With a silky voice that chilled Forenk, the malkaloki devil said, "Ahhh, You must be the pig boy. We have been waiting for you." He motioned to a corner of the Hetman's house, "Your friends have kept me company."

Tied up against the supporting timbers of the house, their arms above their heads and their ample bodies exposed and bleeding from multiple whip marks, hung his divine guardians, Heela and Donoxa.

"Forenk!" the girls said together, "be careful his magic is strong."

The malkaloki waved his hand and there was silence. Forenk could see the girls moving their mouths but heard no sound.

"I have used your pretty angels and I shall slay them when I am finished toying with them, just like I did with your pig-bitch mother!" said the malkaloki. Even as the demon said the last few words he swung his arm overhead and produced a ball of molten fire that came hurtling at Forenk. Swinging the sword up, Forenk managed to deflect the burning orb, yelping as scalding cinders sparked out from the impact, burned holes through his clothing, and scalded his skin away where ever it hit.

"I have slain the avatar of the hog goddess, captured and used your angel whores," said the malkaloki, sizing up Forenk and tossing a flaming fireball up and down in his hand as if it were a cold stone. Suddenly he swung his other arm back and lashed out with the whip. The whip, which looked very much like a tentacled snake, wrapped itself around Forenk's legs. The malkaloki jerked back on the writhing whip with a flick of his wrist and Forenk fell backwards and lost consciousness for a moment when his head struck the floor with a loud thump.

The malkaloki laughed like a madman and said, “The Hero of Pigland? If they bards compose a lay for you it will be a short tragedy, for your tale ends today!”

The malkaloki threw the flaming orb that he had been juggling in his other hand. Forenk came to just in time to raise the sword in defense. The fireball exploded against the flat side of the blade spraying a shower of burning particles. Forenk screamed sharply as the hot magic embers splashed onto the skin of his face and hands. Red welts showed through his shirt and trousers where the pig skin had been disintegrated.

“Enough toying with you, pathetic pig maggot,” said the malkaloki. The demon held his hands together and then slowly drew them apart. A much larger fireball, than the two previous, materialized between his palms. It was large enough to engulf and roast Forenk.

In desperation Forenk spasmodically threw the sword at the malkaloki. The demon looked stupidly surprised as the blade bit deep into his chest. He looked at Forenk quizzically, as if expecting Forenk to explain the interruption, then he crumpled to his knees and fell face forward into the dirt unceremoniously.

“Nooooooooooo!” a shrill voice in Forenk’s head screeched. He recognized Drogana’s screechy voice in its spirit form. What he did not know was that although Drogana’s spirit was sightless, she could see through the eyes of her squirrel servitors and had seen all that had come to pass, including her failure to slay Forenk and regain the Squirrel Sword.

“Auuuhhhhhh, bastard pig fornicator!” she screamed, “SQUIRREL KIND!” Drogana’s voice commanded in an unholy roar, “COME TO ME!” Throughout the village in every direction and beyond, thousands of squirrels stopped pillaging the village and attacking villagers to come scampering at the witch’s bidding. Using her remaining power Drogana chose the first squirrel to arrive on the spot and possessed it’s tiny body with her vile spirit. This single slavering squirrel now held Drogana’s soul and essense.

When the next squirrel arrived it was absorbed by the first and two became one larger squirrel, then a third squirrel was drawn into the growing squirrel entity, and a forth and as they came the size of the beast continued to grow until it was a titan towering three times the height of Forenk.

Forenk meanwhile suffering from multiple wounds and burns scrambled-crawled towards the dead malkaloki and the Squirrel Sword, whose blade had been pushed through the demon's body when he fell forward and now protruded several feet above his blood stained back.

This squirrel monster was the largest and most horrible of all the evil horrors Forenk had seen. Claws as large as giant bull's horns hung from its paws and buck-toothed fangs the length of Forenk's legs protruded from its lipless mouth. The monster squirrel lumbered, hopping with ground-vibrating leaps to cut off Forenk from reaching the sword.

"Get away from him, you buck-toothed BITCH!" thundered a booming but queenly feminine voice. The form of an enormous animal-hominid materialized out of a quickly forming mist. Forenk turned to stare in awe at the titan. She had a perfect woman's body adorned by two rows of teats that ran from below her neck to her hips. Above the neck sat the snouted head of a pig.

Forenk, still in agony from the bruises and many burns, burns that still let off wisps of smoke, said, "Mother?"

54 A Rhyme With Swine Takes Time

"Yes, sweetheart, did you miss your old mom?" said the goddess. Then she charged the dumbfounded squirrel-monster Drogana. The battle was brief. Thegotta batted Drogana and each time her hand slapped at the squirrel monstrosity gobs of squirrels separated from the form of the monster so that it shrunk each time it was hit. The fight ended when a few surviving squirrels resolved back into their former minuscule shapes and ran off. Drogana's spirit howled as her soul was shredded and obliterated, tattered wisps of her odious essence disappearing into oblivion.

Mojka, Forenk's mother, now in her true form as Thegotta, the Goddess of Pigland, said to her son, "You have returned reborn from the hero's journey. Have not all my words come true? Now you know the truth and have seen the outside world. A very small section of it I may add."

"Yes, mother, and I am in great pain right now," Forenk groaned.

"Yes, well, you always were a bit clumsy, and I can only stay for moments, my son. My mortal body was destroyed by the malkaloki" she said, absentmindedly kicking the dead demon's body through a wall of the hetman's hut and into the sharp spikes of a conveniently propped-up pitchfork outside. The sword fell free of the demon's lifeless body as it whirled past, and landed near Forenk, blade in the ground, pommel upright and facing him.

"Take the sword, my son, and go out into the world. Many adventures await you. Your wounds will mostly heal and the ones that will not will mark you as a veteran of many battles," boomed Thegotta. "I must leave you now, goddesses no longer walk the world freely. You will be the last progenitor of the gods hereabout or so it is written somewhere."

"Mother, do not go! How will I, how can I, what if I need you," pleaded Forenk.

Thegotta let out a sigh of wariness. “Remember my temple in Eysor? Each god has an alcove or cell inside that temple, mine is the big cell on the left. You can stand there and invoke my name. You can call me on my cell.”

“Ow,” said Forenk.

As Thegotta dematerialized Forenk remembered Heela and Donoxa.

“Might want to untie us,” they said. “We will not be able to stay much longer either. We must not set a bad precedent for other divines,” they laughed together as if they were all still casually prancing down an idyllic path somewhere in the wild. “How sweet to see you reunited with your mother, Forenk, and how you have changed since we met. We are proud to have aided you in your quest”

Just then a gang of perniciously scurvy men could be seen as they approached. Forenk thought that he might really meet his end this time until he recognized Black Thumb and his pirates.

“We have come to save the day, arrggg!” said Black Thumb. He had on a black eyepatch, an armless sleeve was pinned up to his shoulder and in his remaining hand he held a crutch that he balanced his single leg and wooden peg leg on.

Forenk managed to wince through the pain and say, “Captain Black Thumb, you are a bit late. What happened to you?”

“Well, I’ve ad a change of art if you must know,” said the pirate captain.

“No, I mean your eye, arm and leg,” said Forenk.

“I moved Drogana’s curse of ill fortune onto Black Thumb on the docks of Eysor,” said Donoxa. “Now that she is no more, her curse is lifted.”

“And,” added Gerojef, walking in and joining the discussion after surviving his own horrendous battle with the squirrels. “I have the sacred relic, the one that the squirrel bit off.” He held up a sack, in shape resembling a single testicle. In his other hand he held the ancestor squirrel’s tail that Heela had chopped off before Forenk killed the Sacred Squirrel.

“Can we put it back on?” asked Forenk, referring to the sack.

“Errrm, err, maybe we could, let me think. Hmmm, well maybe there could be a chance, no, that would not work. So no, definitely not,” said Gerojef.

From where she stood, arms tied above her head to the supporting timber of the hetman’s hut while the pirates looked on lasciviously, Donoxa said, “I m hungry.”

“Me, too,” said Heela.

The End

The Places and Peoples of Pigland

• Ancestor Squirrel

The spirit of one of the first created squirrels, inhabiting the body of a living squirrel in the time of Forenk's career. This reincarnated rodent repeatedly plagued Forenk, trying to bite off his nuts to prevent him from propagating his father's, Mipinus, line of progeny.

• Blahstwort

A pinkish tuber shaped plant which when prepared by boiling it to a sludge, produces a balm which causes extreme itchiness and diarrhea.

• Donoxa

One of the two angels of fecundity, one of magic, one of war, sent to aid Forenk on his quest of discovery.

• Drogana

A powerful witch spirit, the local Goddess of Revenge and wife of Jykee.

• Eysor

The largest and filthiest city of Pigland is also one of the famed cities of degeneracy and just brimming with loafers, hookers and shoe salesmen. Aside from the porcine staples, the main exports of this commercial center are shoes, sociopathic drifters and social diseases. Eysor is home to the only temple in the region. It is dedicated to the pantheon of local deities. Admittedly, the Gods here are not that impressive, their powers on the average equaling those of circus performers, especially clowns. The worshiper denizens of Eysor can be summed up as "one sorry lot," and almost uniformly non-distinguished and undesirable.

• Floexa

Hetman Walla's daughter and the most attractive female in the village of Pig Whistle.

• Floob

A wise man and fortune teller of the village of Pig Whistle.

• Ghostbane

A a pinkish tuber-shaped plant that enables communication with the spirit world and burns ghosts as fire will a living mortals. It merely needs to be rubbed into the skin to allow a subject to commune with the dead. It can be rubbed on weapons which makes the arms effective against spirits.

• Harbo

Forenk's family's prize pig.

• Heela

One of the two angels of fecundity, one of magic, one of war, sent to aid Forenk on his quest of discovery.

• Hetman Walla

The chieftain of the village of Pig Whistle.

• Hezfytis

Oracle of Swine Mt.

• Jykee

A ruling woodland spirit and god of squirrels. Once ruler of the area until defeated by Mipinus.

• Kankehsor

An ancient city, capital of the civilization of the ruined ruins

• Kormed

Mojka's husband and Forenk's adopted father.

• Malkalocki

Progeny of the chaos devil.

• Memus

The place or plane of the gods, which can mesh and intertwine with anywhere in the world.

• Mipinus

The local fertility god, also the god of mud.

• Mojka

The last earthly avatar of the Goddess of Pigland. A lovable but somewhat deformed and mildly demented pig- farming hag.

• Mormoomi

Mother Nereid, Queen of the Sea Nymphs and the daughter of the stars and sea. Renowned for her Oracles.

Mouron

A powerful Wizard whose bad memory has earned him the appellation, "The Stupid Wizard."

• Never Named

A useless expanse of desert, scrub and nondescript wildlife, so uninterestingly forgettable, that no one has bothered to name it.

• Pig Milk

A small tribal farming village culture based on the commerce of pigs. The people there besides being inbred, are ugly, unbathed, uncouth and especially uninspired.

• Pig Whistle

The same as Pig Milk above, but not as impressive. Pigland = An abysmally smelly place.

• Pointless

A broad range of unremarkable hills inhabited by demented hunters, unsuccessful bandits and only an occasional animal (Most of the native wildlife starves to death because they are too stupid to eat)

• Ruined Ruins

The Capital (and only city) of an ancient empire whose most notable, and sole characteristic was the immediate subjugation and enslavement of any beings they came in contact with. It has been pointed out by later historians, that, most civilizations lasting 8000 years have developed inter-stellar space flight, while the folk from the ruins had just finished putting the final touches on the wheel.

• Simori

The Goddess of the Inner Sea, the cradle of rivers.

• Squirrel Turd

A squalid colony of haphazardly constructed dwellings and its pathetic inhabitants. The collection of formless dung hovels and sickly humanoid forms whose lack of recognizable traits denoting civilization prevented it or them from being properly classified as a village or culture.

• Tahleos

The God of Stars, Father Fate.

• The Forest (of Trees)

An undistinguished glade, totally unpopulated by anything worthwhile. Even squirrels shun the place.

• The Sacred Grove

A sacred grove.

• The Sea

A seemingly endless body of salt water. Seafarers occasionally recall legends that might have happened, or at least someone suggested that they might have happened, but these stories are too stupid, boring and pointless to be retold here.

• The Stupid Wizard's Tower

This piece of architecture's entertainment value is that the sole resident managed while working on the secret of immortality though nights of the arcane ritual and esoteric study to lock himself in the tower and leave the key in the door on the outside. In the oft recited song it is noted that he should have tackled the Open Portal spell first.

• Thungi

A warrior monk of The Order of the Oracle of Swine Mountain.

• Toobang

The amorous tanner of Pig Whistle.

• Ugly

A stretch of unattractive sandy beaches somehow lacking any trace of natural beauty. A non-place whose almost painful monotony is broken only by an occasional outcropping of rock or cliff face even more unsightly than the beach.

* Yore Glyphs

Representational symbols of true speech, the first tongue and the language used by the gods.

• Zondak Zook

The wizard Mouron's familiar, a hill dwarf or halfolk spirit from the Mountains of Heaven.

www.ingramcontent.com/pod-product-compliance
Lightning Source LLC
Chambersburg PA
CBHW070558120726
47909CB00007B/2381
* 9 7 8 0 6 9 2 3 5 9 9 5 2 *